Nothing's Sweeter than Candy

LOTCHIE BURTON
author of *Prelude to a Seduction*

Crimson Romance
New York London Toronto Sydney New Delhi

CRIMSON
ROMANCE

Crimson Romance
An Imprint of Simon & Schuster, Inc.
1230 Avenue of the Americas
New York, NY 10020

ISBN 978-1-4405-8908-9
ISBN 978-1-4405-8909-6 (ebook)

To Antwan Burton and Angela Burton. A mother couldn't ask for a better or more supportive son, or a more perfect daughter-in-law. The two of you belong together, and I'm so very glad you both belong to me.

To Cathy Ray, Patricia (Patty) Pugh, Denise Jackson, and Zaida Martin. Thank you all for your continued support and encouragement, and for giving me your time and helpful advice. And a special thanks to you, Patty, for pushing me so hard to work on this book and complete it. If not for your relentless insistence that I stop procrastinating, it might still be sitting on my hard drive.

To Kurt, my very enthusiastic friend and editor. Thank you for the male perspective.

Chapter 1

Candace Brown stood in the hotel lobby staring at the row of elevators, hesitant to push the button that would take her to the upper levels. Nash, her once-in-a-blue-moon lover had called. He'd said he was in town, but only for the night. Her "if you had any sense" inner voice had shrieked *bad idea* as soon as she'd hung up the phone. But every woman alive knows raging hormones and no sex for months will kick a sensible thought in its ass, and trample it right into the dust.

She'd rushed out the door, jumped in her car, and driven there at breakneck speed, ready for a long-overdue romp between the sheets. Now with only an elevator ride standing between her and satisfying the ache between her legs, that nagging voice reemerged and refused to be ignored. And it told her she was about to take stupid to a whole other level. Suddenly she was undecided.

In the few months she'd known him, he'd never shown a capacity to care about other human beings or feel real emotion. There wasn't a sensitive, civilized bone in his body. Lately, he'd started the annoying habit of calling her "Freak." He claimed it was a term of endearment, but the unpleasant way the word rolled off his tongue felt more like accusation than kindness. She loathed the way it made her feel. Nash enjoyed using offensive, demeaning language to make her uncomfortable and feel less like a woman and more like an object.

Basically, Andrew Nash was an asshole. He'd weaseled his way into her life using his affable charm, a trait she'd quickly learned was pure gimmick. Her first mistake was agreeing to go out with him, immediately followed by her second: going to bed with him. And she'd continued falling into bed with him again and again, all while ignoring her better judgment and ditching her sense of pride.

So why did she keep coming back? Because he was handsome and fit, and in spite of his asinine behavior, the man knew his way around a woman's body. His hands and mouth flowed like pure magic over every inch of her—pushing her buttons, plucking her cords, and playing her like a fine-tuned instrument. Aware of his abilities and her weaknesses, he skillfully used both to manipulate her and turn her inside out. When she was with him, she *was* the freak he'd named her—he knew exactly how to make her lose control. It pissed her off that the man who let loose her deepest inhibitions took such great pleasure in mocking her for it.

The fact that Candace's lust for Nash far outweighed her self-respect hadn't mattered until now. So what had changed? Why hadn't she pushed that elevator button? Maybe she'd finally grown tired of his demeaning comments and deliberate disrespect. Maybe the sex wasn't worth the insults. Maybe it was time to stop settling for temporary satisfaction while enduring constant humiliation. While struggling to make her choice, she was distracted by her reflection in the highly polished chrome of the elevator doors. The sight stirred up a startling memory; the walls and sounds of the lobby melted away, replaced by a more powerful and provoking image.

All of a sudden she was with Nash, standing before a long bank of windows as high as the ceiling, staring back at their reflection in the tinted sheets of glass. The world beyond was muted and shrouded in darkness, illuminated solely by pinpoints of artificial light that flickered in distant windows or flashed by in the street way down below. The room was nearly as dark, dimly lit with soft lighting that spilled over from an adjacent room. Their naked bodies were cast in silhouette and posed on full display in front of the window, where they stood uncaring and unashamed.

She leaned back and relaxed her body into his, her hips and thighs cradled against him. She gave in to the tingling sensations created by caressing hands that glided over her sensitive skin in long, sensual strokes. Hands that swept across her shoulders, down her back, and reached underneath her breasts, cupping and lifting them high. Molded around her full and swaying flesh, his fingers pulled and pinched her distended nipples hard, sending electrical shivers down her spine. Warm, moist breath pushed through her curls and tantalized her ear and neck. His wet tongue probed her ear and teased her neck and throat, seeking the soft, telltale sounds of pleasure as proof that she craved his touch.

He pressed her tightly against him, fusing them together and pulling her back against his stiff arousal. The coarse hairs on his thighs and pelvis chafed against the soft skin of her bare back and bottom, the friction tormenting her. He bent her forward doggy-style in front of the window and moved his body seductively over hers, rubbing against her entrance before easing his stiff length into her waiting wetness. They shared the titillating sensation of penetration, the electrifying feeling of his steel sliding through her satin. Their bodies quivered in pleasure from the intimate joining, his cock encircled by her liquid heat.

Immersed in the moment, they wordlessly watched their bodies in motion, reflected in the glass. She saw through half-closed lids the paleness of his white skin against her darker complexion, and shuddered as his shaft moved with a slow, steady rhythm, in and out between her slick, silken folds. Together they moved in one fluid motion like partners in a private dance, pulling apart and meeting in the middle with force and fervor, again and again. Overcome by nearly unbearable sensations, she alternately welcomed the pleasure and fought against the building ache that would too soon take her over the edge. Fiery heat poured through her veins and scorched and burned her from the inside. The warmth surged and bubbled up into her throat as she soared inevitably toward climax, and emerged as the sound a woman makes on the verge of losing control.

His pace quickened and became more forceful. He pulled her up and pushed her hard against the window and pressed her face and breasts into the glass, her arms splayed out to her sides. Her back arched deeper and her legs spread wider to accommodate his furious and repeated plunges inside her velvet channel. She was lost in passion, overcome by sensation. Approaching the edge of his climax, he grabbed a handful of her hair, yanked her head back, and wrapped his arm around her waist. He pulled her down and pounded her again and again with his thrusting cock. His fingers unerringly found her throbbing clit and furiously rubbed against her sensitive flesh until she erupted in an orgasm so strong she staggered and nearly crumpled to the floor ...

The buzzing sound of her phone vibrating in her purse interrupted her brief, yet vivid recollection. The caller ID told her it was Nash.

"Hello?"

"Hey, Freak. I've been waiting for over an hour. Where are you?"

Her jaw tightened. Instant clarity flooded her indecisive mind, and common sense demanded to be heard. There wasn't a damn thing between her and Nash except hot sex. They weren't even friends. Their "relationship" was purely physical and based on convenience for her and mockery for him. Suddenly she realized that being the object of ridicule for the sake of good sex was *ridiculous*.

A dull red shade of anger spread across her cheeks. This was it. This was her wakeup call. She wasn't taking any more crap from Andrew Nash, no matter how good he was in bed.

"I'm not coming."

"You're not coming? Yeah, right." He laughed in sarcastic disbelief. "That's a good one, Freak. So where are you?" he continued. "The nights a-wasting, and I've got plans for that freaky brown-sugar ass of yours."

"I said I'm not coming. I'm not taking any more of your shit. You may be a good fuck, Nash, but that's the only 'good' thing about you. I'm ending this while I still have some of my dignity intact. Sorry for the short notice, but I know you won't have any trouble replacing me with some other freak."

"Look, Freak, I'm not in the mood for games." His voice took on an angry edge. "Get your ass over here. If you keep me waiting too long, I might have to spank that pretty brown ass, just to teach you a lesson."

The mere mention of the promised spanking made her weak in the knees. A gush of liquid desire soaked her underwear—and pissed her off even more.

"You're an asshole, Nash," she hissed through clenched teeth.

"Yeah, I know." He laughed harshly. "But you're gonna show. We both know you're a fucking addict, and I'm your drug."

Candace viciously stabbed the "end call" button on her phone, walked swiftly back toward the hotel entrance, and gave the valet her ticket. Still fuming when her car arrived, she handed the young man a generous tip and silently celebrated her small victory by charging the parking fee to the asshole's room.

Chapter 2

Candace picked up the phone. "Doctor Jeffers's office, how may I help you?"

"Hi, Candy, is Joyce in?" Candace smiled at the sound of Sarona's voice. She, Joyce, and Sarona had been friends for years. Joyce and Sarona had met at an airport while waiting for a connecting flight home. The two struck up a conversation over a mutual obsession for designer shoes and handbags. Candace had worked for Joyce part-time while attending college, and Joyce offered her a job once she completed her degree. Now the three were nearly inseparable.

"Hi, Sarona. Yes, she's in. She's with a couple of clients, but she'll be done any minute if you don't mind waiting." Joyce was a relationship/marriage counselor and sometimes sex therapist, and her full client list kept Candace's reception desk very busy.

"No, I don't mind. It'll give me a chance to catch up on the latest gossip. What's new? Have you found a man yet, or are you still doggedly holding onto your 'wild, single, and free' status, refusing to give in to the power of love?"

"Nothing's changed. I'm still living single." Candace laughed. "But I *have* sworn off dating for a while."

"Shut your mouth. I don't believe it. Why?"

"Because, the last guy I was seeing was a jerk. He was great between the sheets, but a total ass on his feet."

"Girl, when are you going to stop hanging out with losers? We both know you can do *so* much better. I swear, sometimes I think you go out of your way to hook up with the worst guys around. You'll never find Mr. Right when you insist on looking for Mr. Wrong." Sarona's voice was filled with exasperation. "You've got so much going for you, Candace. You're beautiful *and* crazy smart. I just know there's a great guy out there somewhere who would love to get to know you, if you gave him half a chance."

"Ah yes, my friend, ever the optimist. Just because you've been lucky in love doesn't mean the rest of us are as fortunate. I've got news for you: the dating pool is pretty shallow, and being 'crazy smart' isn't in high demand."

Candace couldn't find a way out of her predicament. The deep end was filled with puffed-up, self-important egotists who had no idea how to spot a great catch. At the other end were timid, afraid-of-their-own-shadow types, with such fragile egos that a strong-willed, outspoken woman scared the hell out of them. Her choices were either assholes or sheep. The chances of finding a decent, eligible, intelligent bachelor who's able to cope with an independent woman were slim to none.

"So I won't be looking for Mr. Right, Mr. Wrong, or Mr. Anybody for a while. I'm taking off the silk thong and putting on my one hundred percent cotton panties, and I'm going to stock up on batteries and become reacquainted with my vibrator."

"Girl, you are too much." Sarona laughed. "You can be so cynical sometimes."

"Cynicism is only one of my endearing qualities. What about you?" Candace asked, deftly changing the subject. "The last time I heard from you, you were away at a work conference with some guy, and I quote, 'living la vida loca,' and spouting something about 'shouting hallelujah from the rafters.' Care to share the details?"

"I'd love to, but that would require an entire evening complete with wine, cheese and crackers, and assorted chocolates, as well as a notarized agreement not to divulge any or all parts of the conversation."

"Whoa. It was that good?"

"Yeah. It was that good."

"Well, sign me up and swear me in. I can't wait to hear the whole story." At the sound of a door opening, Candace looked up to see Joyce ushering a couple out of her office.

"As always, it's great talking with you, Sarona." She softly chuckled. "But Joyce is available now, so I'll put you through."

"Thanks, Candy. Hey, keep your calendar open. You, Joyce, and I are going to have to get-together when I get back from my trip. It's time for another girls' night out."

"You're going on another trip? This is your third one this month. Joyce won't be happy to hear that. She's already been complaining about all those canceled lunches and happy hours because of you working overtime. She's actually threatened to force you to choose between her or your job."

"Yeah, I know. That's why I'm calling. I have to break the news to her."

"Well, I don't envy you that charming little chore." Candace laughed as she signaled Joyce and pressed a button to transfer the call.

Pulling files and preparing for the next appointment, Candace replayed her conversation with Sarona in her head. It sounded like she'd had quite an adventure during her recent trip, and that was great. But, unfortunately, whenever any of her friends scored big in the game of love, it didn't bode well for her. It meant they'd want to include her in their world of happiness, which always translated into another round of well-meaning meddling and matchmaking. Somewhere along the way, Joyce and Sarona had made it their self-appointed goal in life to find Candace a "Mr. Right." The two were determined that she do what was expected of every woman of a certain age—settle down, start a family, and live happily ever after. Because it was their dream to do so, they thought it was only natural she should feel the same way.

She made a face and cringed at the thought. What was all the fuss about anyway, to rush into marriage and motherhood? For

Christ's sake, she was only twenty-seven. She loved her freedom and celebrated every moment of it. Ever since she'd begun working for Joyce, she'd watched clients come and go, and sometimes come back again. She'd seen firsthand how difficult it was to make a relationship work, and she wanted no part of that drama.

Besides, there ain't no such thing as Mr. Right. Suddenly, her mood rapidly descended into a dark and cynical place. *That man is a fairy tale, just like Santa Claus, trumped up and told solely to little girls.* Ultimately, children grew up and stopped believing in Santa Claus, but little girls became women who never stopped believing in Mr. Right. She'd learned that fairy tales were best left to children, not grown-ass women. Andrew Nash was living and breathing proof of that lie.

She hadn't always been so cynical. She'd once held the same blind belief of all women in search of that one man destined to fulfill their fantasy—until selfish, uncaring men like Nash had dashed her dreams and destroyed her hope. The facts of life opened her eyes to the truth: that not everyone gets a happily-ever-after ending; sometimes all they get is "the end."

Candace stared blankly at the papers spread across her desk, her thoughts anchored in another place and time. Painful memories had been suppressed, but not forgotten. She knew what it was like to be in love. She'd been there, done that—twice. And twice her heart had been broken and handed back to her in pieces.

At sixteen she'd been sweet, sensitive, and naïve, trusting her emotions and believing in the fantasy. She'd given away her heart and her virginity to another sixteen-year-old because of her faith in the fairy tale. She was in love, and love was reason enough to justify her decision. A week later, he was gone. He'd moved on to another girl and left her feeling so hurt, confused, and ashamed that it was hard to breathe. She hid her suffering behind fake smiles and forced laughter, and pretended to agree with others who insisted it was only a teenage crush. Time passed and life went on, and she'd gotten through it. But if it was "only a crush," why did it still hurt at twenty-seven as bad as it had at sixteen?

At twenty-three she'd deliberately pursued relationships with older men, blaming her earlier heartbreak on her immature partner. Age and experience would make all the difference in the world. Wouldn't it? The second love of her life was a dream come true: handsome, sweet, attentive—and a liar. She wasn't the only woman in his life, just one of many he wined, dined, and used for his selfish entertainment. There'd been plenty of warning signs, but she'd chosen to ignore them, stubbornly fighting to hold onto the dream. Eventually, she'd caught him in one too many lies and had to acknowledge another failure. And her belief in forever-after began to unravel.

It didn't matter that the circumstances were different; the pain was the same. She'd sat alone in the dark with the curtains drawn and her face stuffed in a pillow to soak up her tears and muffle the sobs. Then she crawled under the covers, closed her eyes, and wished she could die, just to make the hurt go away. She didn't die. She endured and made a vow. Never, ever, again. That would be the last time she'd serve herself up on a platter, because she'd never survive heartbreak number three. Sure, it was true that time healed all wounds, but wounds deep enough left scars.

After running away from love, she'd locked away her emotions and hardened her heart, turning toward men like Nash. It didn't take a trained psychiatrist to figure out why. Men like that had no hidden agendas. They didn't smile in your face and tell lies to get into your pants. They made sure she knew up front what they were after, and it was her choice whether or not to go along. They'd taught her two important facts of life: love was a game, and men didn't mature with age—they simply got better at playing the game.

There were no rules set in stone; you made them up as you went along. So, she made a few of her own. Rule number one: no expectations, no disappointments. Rule number two: never make a man responsible for her happiness. Subsequently, all her affairs were purely physical, regulated to booty calls and one-night stands. Emotional entanglements only got in the way. Guys operated just fine following this philosophy, so why couldn't she?

She was lucky; her mixed-race heritage made her a curiosity, an exotic oddity, something to "try for the first time," so attracting men was easy. Attracting the wrong man was easier. She dated men from different professions and ethnic backgrounds because she'd always been fascinated by "different." But in the end, it all boiled down to the same thing: it didn't really matter what color a man's skin was—lying, deceiving bastards came in every shade.

Chapter 3

"Hey man, it's Brice. I'm just checking in to see what's going on."

"Everything's cool," David said. "What's up with you?"

"It's all good. I'm glad you made it back okay, but man, you know I've been waiting for the details on how things went down with you and Sarona. I'm anxious to hear how your game plan played out."

Brice Coleman and David Broussard had been friends since their college years. Now both in their mid-thirties, the two had recently become business partners in a software and communications security consulting service. They developed antivirus software for high-profile business corporations and made them aware of cybercrime vulnerabilities. They often hacked their way into the computer databases of potential clients, just to get their attention.

Both were alike in a number of ways: same wealthy family background, same striking good looks and athletic build, and same interests in education and technology. Their only real differences had been in their taste in women, until recently.

David usually went for the blonde-haired, blue-eyed model type, all looks, body, and no brains. His latest infatuation, Sarona Maxwell, was a complete departure from his usual sort: African-American, voluptuous, and intelligent. Unlike David, being attracted to women of color was nothing new for Brice. He'd had an affinity for brown skin in every shade, shape, and form since childhood.

"Yeah, I know." David laughed. "But I'm afraid you might be a little disappointed. Things didn't go exactly as I imagined. Turns out I was no match for Ms. Sarona Maxwell. She beat me at my own game and took my ass down, hard. And I didn't even put up a fight."

"What? Wait, am I hearing you right? Is this the same man who left here a week ago with every intention to seduce the woman who's driving you crazy?"

"Yeah, you heard right. And, no, I'm not the same man. David the Player no longer exists. My player's card has expired, and I don't plan on renewing it."

Brice chuckled at the memory of David's scheme to seduce Sarona. The two of them traveled in the same business circles and attended the same conferences, but rarely interacted. According to David, Sarona was polite, friendly, and funny as hell, but she usually avoided him like the plague. Used to being the center of female attention, David was bothered and intrigued to the point of erotic fantasies, and his sex dreams almost drove him crazy. The more she dodged him, the more determined he was to have her. It was a classic case of "wanting what you can't have."

He'd left town with the intention to use his charm, good looks, and every tactic in the player's handbook to seduce her and fulfill his fantasies. Brice had questioned his judgment on executing his plan away from home, and with such a short time constraint. It had seemed simpler to work his magic here, in Atlanta. But David argued that if Sarona had the home field advantage, she'd also have a million ways to avoid him. At a conference in a hotel on the west coast, hundreds of miles away for a week, there were only so many places she could go to get away from him. No matter how far she ran, she'd always have to come back. And if that didn't work, well, he could use the excuse of a contract proposal to contact her through her company.

But it seemed David's plan had gone just a bit awry.

"That is freaking unbelievable. And scary," Brice choked out. "I mean, I knew you had it bad, but I had no idea it was that bad. I thought you were just obsessing and needed to get laid. The plan was to get her *in* bed and *out* of your system. What the hell happened?"

"I don't know. You're right. I was obsessing, and I did need to get laid. Once the ball started rolling, though, things took off and got away from me. As I tried to seduce her, everything got turned around, and in the end ... well, in the end, I was the one who was seduced. I think I'm in love, man."

"I don't know what to say. I'm floored. I guess I should be happy for you, but God, I hope it's not contagious. I'm in no hurry to get tangled up and tied down by some woman. No offense."

"None taken."

"Damn, I can't believe it. You, of all people."

"I know. I can't believe it either, but I guess it had to happen sooner or later. And for all your blustering denial, don't be surprised when it creeps up on you and bites you in the ass. But don't worry, I'll be the first to hand you a beer, slap you on the back, and say I told you so. I'll welcome you into the brotherhood of the fallen with open arms."

"Screw that. I'm telling you right now—I don't want any part of your 'brotherhood.' Unlike you, my man, there's no way in hell I'm going down without a fight. Anyway, I also called to tell you I've scheduled an appointment for next week at Peterson, Powell, and Lambert. Our sales department made the pitch a few days ago, but the IT director wanted a personal interview with one of the partners, so I'm going in to close the deal. But by all rights, we both know it should be you, since it was your idea to approach the company in the first place. It was your, what did you call it, 'backup plan,' right?"

"Yeah, well, even though I no longer need a fallback plan, that contract is still good for business. I'll have a lot of explaining to do once Sarona finds out about that little gem of an idea. By the way, I'll be leaving the business in your capable hands once again because I'm taking off for another couple of weeks. I'll check out your report when I get back, but right now, all I care about is spending time getting up close and personal with my woman."

"All right man, no problem," Brice said. "Enjoy your trip."

Brice disconnected his call in a state of shock. David's news had totally blown him away. His friend had fallen. Hard. The whole idea was surreal and unbelievable, and it had him worried. Where would David's departure from bachelorhood leave him? What was he supposed to do now, without his wingman? The two of them had made a great team: handsome, eligible, and on the prowl, enjoying the spoils of female conquest. They looked out for each other and steered likely prospects in the other's direction. Neither had seen the advantage in settling for one woman when there were so many as yet untapped resources. Now with David suddenly out of the picture, he'd be on his own, flying solo.

Brice had grown up the son of a U.S. diplomat. His father had once held appointments in countries all over the world, and at a young age Brice had been exposed to many different cultures. As a boy, he'd been fascinated by the differences in the skin color and texture of darker children. When he grew into an adolescent and his hormones were running rampant, he found himself more attracted to females of other races than those of his own. It wasn't something he could explain. It was simply something he felt, strongly and internally. His free-spirited parents never questioned the friends he brought home or the girls he preferred to date. They didn't try to influence him one way or the other, allowing him to find his own way.

His fascination followed him into adulthood, and he began dating Latina and African American women exclusively. He was drawn to strong, beautiful, exotic women, and he liked the in-your-face attitude, fire, and spice he encountered from women with diverse cultural backgrounds. A strong-willed man, he needed a woman who could handle and counterbalance his sometimes-domineering nature. But even though he was a take-charge kind of guy, his mother had raised him to respect women. Her love and strength had molded him, and she would kick his ass big time if he ever said or did anything disrespectful toward a woman.

Brice was a multifaceted man with many interests. He loved music, computers, and, of course, women, approaching each of these interests with purpose and intensity. The musician in him was a perfectionist, constantly in search of those elusive musical notes that would bring his songs to perfection. The man in him strove for erotic encounters that had the same depth of feeling and flow as good music. His carnal appetites were voracious, but kept under strict control. He rarely allowed his passionate nature to surface. Exposure to his deepest desires would probably frighten your average romance-seeking, immersed-in-fantasy, vanilla-sex-loving female away.

He knew what women saw when they looked at him: handsome, successful ... and a meal ticket. He was a free ride to the good life. He didn't begrudge them for wanting to use him to advance their social status. It was only natural. So what if he had to give up a few trinkets and an expensive meal or two. When it was all said and done, they both got what they wanted out of the deal and moved on. He didn't hang around long enough to chance getting involved in anything serious. He'd let them use his body and his money, for a time, but he'd never be fool enough to give them his heart. *That* was off-limits for all the money-hungry, status-seeking, survival-of-the-fittest social climbers.

Even though he was a typical man, trying to rack up as many points as he could before the game was over, he still had an old-fashioned streak in him. He was holding out for someone special—the one who made his stomach churn, his blood burn, and his heart damn near stop beating. Someone interested in experiencing sex and intimacy in new and exciting ways. And most important of all, she'd accept him "as is" and wouldn't spend the rest of their lives trying to change him or turn him into something he could never be. *Now* that's *probably a fantasy*. But if dreams could come true for someone like David, the ultimate playboy, then maybe there was hope for Brice yet.

Chapter 4

Brice was nearly thirty minutes early for his meeting. He'd learned early on that timing was everything, and he made it a point to always be at the right place at the right time. Today would prove to be no exception to his rule.

At the end of the hall was an impressive mahogany wraparound desk occupied by a petite and attractive brunette. Glancing at the nameplate displayed on the desk, Brice smiled and introduced himself.

"Good morning, Ms. Johnston. My name is Brice Coleman. I'm here for a ten o'clock appointment with Mr. Charles Chancellor."

"Good morning, Mr. Coleman," she responded cheerfully. "I'll let Mr. Chancellor's secretary know you're here." He waited while she made the call.

"Mr. Chancellor is currently in a meeting, which should be ending shortly. In the meantime, you're welcome to have a seat."

"Sure. I can do that."

Eyeing a recent copy of *Sports Illustrated,* he picked it up and began riffling through the pages, occasionally glancing up at the clock on the wall.

While absently turning pages, his ears picked up on a distant, distinct, and confident click of high heels tapping against the hard marble flooring. The sound grew louder as it came nearer, and a primal instinct as old as time instantly kicked into heightened awareness. Brice pretended to be engrossed in the magazine while anxiously awaiting the arrival of those as-yet-unseen heels. Timing was everything.

At the exact moment the sound breezed past his chair, his eyes rose to catch sight of a stunning pair of long, café-latte-brown legs sashaying by. His gaze traveled up their length and came to rest on a gorgeous round bottom, covered by a short-fitted skirt that swayed slowly from side to side in perfect sync with some erotic, unheard melody.

With his interest piqued, he quickly forgot the magazine in his hands. He covertly watched the woman's purposeful, easy-flowing gait as she headed straight for the reception desk. Lucky for him, she stopped directly in front and afforded him an unobstructed view of her stunning backside. He had yet to see her face, but the view from behind was remarkable.

Her figure was long and lithe, and her shapely bottom stood high and firm above toned, muscular legs. They looked as though they belonged to a dancer or an athlete—and strong enough to squeeze a man tight as they wrapped around his waist, holding on and pulling him in deep. His cock stirred and twitched unexpectedly. Her heels were at least four inches high and accentuated the curve of her hips, the dip of her back, and the width of her shoulders. A full, springy, spiraling, reddish-blonde mane of hair stood out and hung low, brushing her neck and shoulders. She wore a two-piece custom-tailored suit in a rich, dark plum. Brice held his breath and waited expectantly.

"Good morning, Sylvia. How are you doing today?"

When Brice heard the first musical strains of her voice—a sound of unadulterated fantasy laced with seduction and steeped in sex—his immediate response was purely physical. His balls crawled up into his groin as his shaft thickened and tightened.

"Oh my goodness, Candace Brown! What a surprise. We haven't seen you around here in a while." Sylvia was obviously delighted to see her. "If you're here to see Sarona, she's not here. She's out of town. Again."

"Yes, I know." Candace laughed, and an electrical shock swept through Brice's body and made his hair stand on end. Musical notes danced in his head, and a pageantry of colors pulsed and glowed behind his eyes. Other musicians had described this euphoric phenomenon, of sound taking the form of indescribable emotion and color. He'd never believed in such a thing, until now. *And* God, *what a rush.* The mention of Sarona's name added to his excitement, and he wondered how well they knew one another.

"Actually I'm here to pick up some forms she left behind for Dr. Jeffers. Sarona said she'd leave them with her secretary. Could you buzz her and let her know I'm here?"

"Sure, but she's not in her office right now. I saw her heading for the supply department about ten minutes ago. She'll probably be back any minute. If you like, you can have a seat and wait."

"Okay, thanks."

Brice's heart pounded, his groin throbbed, and the rest of him damn near melted in his seat as he waited anxiously to see the face behind the voice. When she turned, every intention of making a covert assessment deserted him. He was staring. He knew he was staring, but he couldn't help himself. She was stunning, with her lovely brown skin and tawny tresses that spiraled and curled about her face, neck, and shoulders. Her face was a perfect oval shape with high cheekbones, a button nose, and very full, very sensuous lips. Her eyes, large and catlike, were the color of light-brown honey and sparkled with tiny flecks of gold. Fringed with long lashes beneath perfectly arched brows, they twinkled with humor and intelligence.

All at once, an inexplicable need welled up and rushed through him—an urge to plunge his hands into her hair, run his tongue over that gorgeous brown skin, and hear her melodious voice purr with pleasure.

But the urgent need for self-preservation pulled him back from an invisible edge. His gut churned. This intense, unexpected attraction tripped off alarm bells inside his head. He knew intuitively this woman could potentially change the carefree life he knew and loved. The set of his jaw became as hard as steel and his mood transformed from charged, overheated, and excited to tense and agitated.

Brice openly watched as Candace strode past and took a seat several spaces over. As the smell of her perfume wafted in the air, his remaining senses surrendered to this unexpected and unsettling stranger.

• • •

When Candace turned, her eyes were immediately drawn to the handsome, dark-haired man sitting directly across from the receptionist's desk. His bluish-black, medium-length hair fell rakishly across his forehead, cut in a loosely tapered style that accented his rugged features. He had a broad brow and nose, high cheekbones, a squared chin with a dimple, and full thick lips. His skin was a sun-kissed bronze with natural olive undertones, and even though seated, he looked to be more than six feet tall. He was dressed in a tailored Armani in dark charcoal gray, a royal-blue shirt, and a blue-and-black patterned silk tie. With broad shoulders, long limbs, and a trim torso, he looked like he'd stepped directly from the pages of *GQ* magazine.

He didn't have the typical "pretty boy" good looks that usually caught her interest. He looked raw, hard. Made of steel. He may have been dressed like a corporate elite ready to mingle with CEOs and presidents, but there was something about the glint in his eye that said *bad boy on a leash*. His Clark Kent disguise might fool corporate, but she'd bet real money that that suit was hiding something absolutely "super" beneath its fine lines and perfect creases.

She suddenly felt the full force of a piercing stare from his beautiful, aquamarine-blue eyes. Eyes that blatantly traveled over her face and body, lingering long enough to make her blush.

She returned the man's open gaze with an equally direct and probing look. As she watched, his unguarded interest and curiosity slowly turned unnervingly defiant and hostile. Her back stiffened, and she moved swiftly past this suddenly intimidating man to take a seat.

• • •

"Candy Girl!" Brice watched as a man with a booming voice approached from the elevators, his arms spread wide in welcome. "Well, aren't you a sight for sore eyes."

Candace smiled broadly. "It's great to see you, too, Paul. Where have you been, out playing golf? You look especially golden brown today," she teased as she gave him a firm, lingering hug.

Brice was consumed with an inexplicable jealousy as he witnessed the intimate contact and easy, familiar laughter. *Who is that old fart?* he thought, annoyed at the idea there might be something more than friendship between the two. *He's old enough to be her father.* Witnessing their embraces and conspiratorial smiles, his stomach twisted and clenched with immediate dislike for the man. He was irritated beyond reason, even more so because he knew his reaction was irrational. Though the entire incident couldn't have lasted more than ten minutes, for Brice it was a long and torturous ten minutes.

Chapter 5

Candace got back to her office a little after lunch. She placed the package in Joyce's inbox and checked the day's appointment schedule. Her morning detour had put her slightly behind, but she'd been happy to see Paul Lambert. Paul and her father were close friends. She'd seen him around the house so often while growing up that he was sort of like an adopted uncle.

After a couple of hours of nonstop work, the face of the handsome stranger from her morning trip popped into her head. She recalled every detail regarding the sexy stranger with the unwavering, penetrating stare and his blue-green eyes that went from burning hot to freezing cold. He had emanated all the qualities of a pure alpha male: roaring confidence, power, and sex appeal. *Now that is the stuff fantasies are made of.* She wondered what his smile would look like. Would that disturbing sheet of ice in his eyes melt into aquamarine blue, if touched with the excitement of desire?

Drifting away and suddenly lost in fantasy, she imagined him towering over her. The warmth of his hands scorched her wrists as he held them high above her head. His weight, heavy and immovable, pushed her up against the wall. He leaned down and nuzzled her neck, pressing his knee between her legs and brushing back and forth across her pulsing and aching nub. Her skirt was hiked up and bunched around her hips, allowing the rough fabric of his jeans to rub against her panty-clad mound. A million volts of electricity raced through her system and short-circuited her brain. She groaned and ground herself against his knee, pushing down hard, desperately in need of that persistent pressure to ease the ache.

As he leaned into her for their first kiss, the swollen evidence of his desire throbbed and pressed intimately against her. His rigidity was welcomed, wanted. Necessary. He held her head immobile and plunged his tongue in and out of her mouth, dueling with her tongue and pulling it into the hot, moist cavern of his own. His kiss robbed her of her senses, branded her with his taste, and marked her with his scent. His free hand traveled over the curve of her bottom and gripped and squeezed it tight, then slid effortlessly under the elastic and up between her thighs ... his tongue and fingers magically stroking and teasing her into a red-hot inferno ...

Her pulse raced as fantasy became entangled with reality. For one brief moment, she didn't know where the hell she was. *Damn, girl, you need to get a grip. Or better yet, get laid.* Candace angrily pushed away from her desk, picked up a stack of files, and headed to the file room. There she spent the rest of the afternoon, buried in work, fighting the urge to wander off again into an erotic fantasyland with the Ice King.

• • •

"Dr. Jeffers's office, how may I help you?" Candace's cheerful greeting was met with silence on the other end of the line. "Hello? May I help you?" she repeated. Half a heartbeat passed, and then a familiar, sneering voice broke the silence.

"What's up, Freak?"

Her blood went cold. *Nash.*

"Hello, Nash. This is a surprise. How did you get this number?"

"Oh, come on. In this age of technology and social media, how could you even ask such a stupid question? I can find out anything I want to know about you, Freak: your number, where you live, who your friends are—even who you sleep with." His voice had a low and nasty quality that sent fingers of unease tingling down her spine. She kept her reply cool and indifferent.

"Of course you can, Nash. I just find it hard to believe that you'd even want to. You made it perfectly clear you could have any freak you wanted, so why bother with this freak?"

"Oh, I want to. No woman walks out on me." There was a brief silence, and then, "Been lonely lately? I know you ain't getting any. That's got to be pretty hard—a woman like you needs to be fucked regularly."

"Have you been *spying* on me?"

"Let's just say I know how to keep track of what's mine. Your pussy belongs to me. I own it. If you weren't still strung out, you would have tried to replace me by now. Go ahead and admit it. You miss me, don't you, Freak?" His voice changed to a husky, sensual whisper. "You can't deny it. I know you still want me. Don't you remember lying in my bed, how I kissed your body and licked you all over with my hot, wet tongue?"

Her nipples beaded involuntarily, and the fine hairs on her arms stood up as her flesh prickled with goose bumps.

"Maybe I should remind you." He breathed heavily into the phone. "I started with your neck, at that spot just behind your ear, and licked you all the way down to your breasts." The sound of his voice teased her with memories that made her core ache and throb. "When I reached those pretty, pert nipples, I sucked and pulled on them and bit down hard enough to make you moan."

Candace clutched the handle of the phone until her fingers cramped.

"Then I played with that ring in your belly button, my tongue going in and out, licking and teasing you and making you wait, and anticipate how much lower I was going to go."

A groan rose in her throat and pushed through her lips.

"Yeah, that's it, Freak. You remember." He continued his torment with a note of implied intimacy. "You remember how I pushed my face way down low and traced your naked lips with my tongue, licking and sucking your clit and tasting your sweet cream."

Candace sucked in a breath and shivered. Her body caught fire, the flames fed by the sound of his voice and the memory of his touch.

"I wrapped my arms around your hips and pulled you closer and spread you wide and stroked my tongue in deep so I could eat you up."

Her clit pulsed with the familiar ache of expectation.

"Do you remember how hot my mouth felt as it made you wet and then sucked you dry? Do you, Freak?"

She bent forward, clutched her groin, and clamped her knees together in a futile attempt to stop the flood of warmth. And to her shame, the heat—unbearable and unstoppable—rushed over and through her, pouring out in moist release, dampening her underwear. A whimpering sound she couldn't suppress slipped out.

"Yeah! That's it, Freak. *I* have the last word. It's not over until I say it's over. Remember that." Nash hung up the phone. The vengefulness in his voice as he severed the connection quashed the fire in her loins and rekindled her anger.

"Ass!" She slammed the receiver down and seethed. Joyce stepped out of her office just in time to witness her furious response.

"Friend of yours?"

"Obscene caller," she responded through clenched teeth.

"Honey, how 'obscene' was it?"

"Don't worry, Joyce. I took care of it. Now, if you'll excuse me, I have to go to the ladies' room." Candace got up and practically ran to the restroom, leaving Joyce to stare after her.

Chapter 6

Brice couldn't get her out of his head, that woman with the sexy body and beautiful face. The unforgettable sound of her voice had lodged itself deep in his memory, and he replayed it over and over again. It spilled like cool water over his skin and down his spine, pooling at the base of his groin and making him as hard as a rock. He'd been like that ever since he'd first heard her speak, nearly twenty-four hours ago. And for twenty-four hours, no matter what he tried—short of yanking out his dick and jerking off— he couldn't make the feeling go away. He was suffering from the hard-on from hell.

He closed his eyes. His hands moved lightly over his saxophone, fingering the keys and caressing its tapered form. The exercise was meant to soothe, but so far it wasn't working. Because of her, notes of perfect clarity rang in his ears and danced in his head, searching for a way out. Finally, he brought the saxophone to his lips, settled his fingers upon the keys, and started to play.

His fingers moved as if they had a mind of their own. There was no hesitation. No uncertainty. No struggling to get it right. The notes came straight from his soul. Her face appeared like a ghostly mist, then melted and blended seamlessly into the sound that flowed from the instrument. The sweet seductive rhythm of her voice, the sway of her body, and the glow of her skin were all captured and entwined in the melody. Through the chaos in his mind, he poured every ounce of anger, uncertainty, and fear he felt bottled up inside of him into the tune.

When the last note was played and the lingering echo had died, Brice laid his saxophone across his knees and sat back. He'd never experienced anything like that before. Never had his music flowed so smooth or sounded so sweet. He'd never allowed himself to feel so empty or so free. Shaking with excitement, he picked up a pen and hurriedly put the song down on paper. An hour later he had a completed first draft, which he promptly titled "Nothing's Sweeter than Candy."

Sweet, sweet candy. His aching cock jumped, and his mouth watered. He licked his lips. He shut his eyes and imagined plunging his hands into that thick mane of hair, pulling her closer to gaze into her golden, honey-brown eyes. He buried his face in her neck and inhaled deeply. She wrapped her arms around his waist and dragged him closer, aligning their bodies. He felt the firm rounded flesh of her breasts imprinted against his chest, and the intimate pressure of her nipples tight and pointed with desire. Her hand crept down and wrapped itself around his hardened cock, gripping and stroking it, back and forth over its length. The feeling of her grasping hand over the rough texture of his jeans was a deadly combination that threatened to make him explode. He took her mouth in a demanding kiss and shamelessly begged for more ...

Brice ran his hands through his hair and down his face in sheer frustration. "There's a disturbance in the force," he mumbled. He could try to ignore the feeling, but he knew himself too well. Once his mind latched onto a problem, he'd find no peace until he'd solved it. If there was any hope of getting her out of his head, he needed to know more. Who she was and what kind of power she wielded.

He had a place to start; he'd overheard everything he needed to know. He knew the person she'd come to see, whom she worked for, and her name. Sure, it might be easier to just call David and have him ask Sarona, but he didn't want to interrupt their romantic vacation. And he didn't want to answer any unwanted questions such a call might generate. Finding her wouldn't be a problem; he breached corporate security for a living, after all. The problem would be what to do after he'd found her. He picked up the phone and waited until the cheerful voice of Sylvia Johnston answered on the other end. "Peterson, Powell, and Lambert, how may I direct your call?"

"Hello, Ms. Johnston? This is Brice Coleman. We met yesterday when I was there for a meeting with Mr. Chancellor."

"Hello, Mr. Coleman, how can I help you?"

"To be honest, I'm not sure if you can, but you're the only person I can think of who might be able to point me in the right direction. You see, I stopped by again yesterday, late afternoon, to drop off additional papers for Chancellor's signature. I haven't heard back from him yet, so I'm a little worried. I hate to admit this, but I got a little confused with the labeling on the drop boxes, and I'm beginning to think I may have left them for the wrong office. I might have left them at Ms. Sarona Maxwell's office instead. I was wondering if you could give me the name of her secretary so that I could ask after the paperwork? It's important that those documents get to Mr. Chancellor by today."

"Of course, I'd be glad to," Sylvia answered. "Her name is Cynthia Burrows. I can transfer you to her office."

"That would be super. Thanks."

"It's not a problem. Good luck."

Brice waited for someone to pick up on the other line.

"Department of Human Resources, this is Ms. Burrows."

"Good morning, Ms. Burrows. My name is Brice Coleman. I'm an IT representative for the business firm Security Matters."

"Good morning, Mr. Coleman, how can I help you?

Brice explained his "situation" and asked her to check her file boxes for papers with the Security Matters title and logo.

"Yes. Just give me a moment, please."

Of course she wouldn't find anything; the query was merely a ruse to ask the follow-up question, the real purpose for his call. "Mr. Coleman?"

"Yes?"

"I'm sorry, but I'm unable to locate any such documents. Perhaps you took them to the right office, after all."

"Okay. That's a relief. Well, thank you for your time. I'll check there next. Um, Ms. Burrows?"

"Yes?"

"I'm sorry to bother you further, but maybe you could help me with another matter?"

"I'll try."

"Yesterday, I spoke with another visitor, a Ms. Candace Brown. She mentioned that her boss might have a potential interest in security upgrades, and we exchanged business cards. At the risk of sounding like a complete idiot, I'm sorry to say that now I can't locate her card. She mentioned she was there to see you, so I was hoping you might have her employer's contact information. I guess I wasn't on top of my game yesterday, but I can't afford to lose a possible client because of a misplaced business card."

"That's not a problem, Mr. Coleman. I know Candace and her employer quite well. Her name is Dr. Joyce Jeffers." She read him the office phone number.

"Thanks again, Ms. Burrows. Have a nice day."

"You're welcome."

That was too easy, Brice thought as he hung up the phone. Who knows? In spite of the cloak-and-dagger routine, this Dr. Jeffers might even turn out to be a potential client. *Hell, if David can use the business as a cover to get close to a woman, then why can't I?*

• • •

"Good morning, Candace," Joyce sang as she strolled into the office.

"Good morning, boss-lady." Candace looked up from her desk with raised eyebrows. "You're in early. Your first patient isn't due until noon."

"Yes, I know, and you can wipe that surprised look off your face right now. For your information, I need to catch up on paperwork. It's been a busy week, and I've fallen behind on a few of my evaluations. Is there any coffee? Please tell me there's coffee. Being up and about this early puts my nervous system into a state of shock."

"Of course there's coffee. I'm always prepared, especially for bosses who show up unexpectedly. There are donuts, too."

Joyce was a tall woman with a slender frame. She had a rich, mocha chocolate chip-brown complexion with soft, smooth features, full lips, and almond-shaped eyes that turned slightly upward. Her appearance denoted a touch of Asian ancestry. Her hair was chestnut brown, thick, short, and twisted in tiny curls that spiraled and sprang out in all directions. Her features were exotic and unique, and she knew exactly how to use them to her advantage. Though she was in her mid-forties, she could easily pass for someone ten to twelve years younger.

"Bless you, child. I don't know what I'd do without you." Joyce put aside her briefcase and purse and filled a cup with coffee, cream, and sugar, "I've got some wonderful news to tell you. You'll be so proud of me. I took a call late yesterday after you'd left. I don't usually, but for some odd reason it didn't go to voice mail, and the ringing was getting on my nerves. Anyway, the call was from a Mr. Coleman. He said he worked for a computer security service and that his company worked by referral. And lucky me, someone referred my office to his business.

"The poor man tried delivering his sales pitch and explaining the miracle of what his service could do for me, but I told him to save his breath. I politely informed him that I didn't speak 'computer-ese' and that my translator had left for the day. I advised that if he wanted to introduce his product to this business, he needed to speak to my resident computer expert. And since I don't actually have one of those," she continued with an airy lilt in her voice as she choose a cinnamon swirl sweet roll, "that my dear, would be you. I told him if he could sell what he's pedaling to my 'computer expert,' then he could consider it a done deal. I suggested he call back during our regular office hours and make an appointment."

Candace simply shook her head and laughed. It wasn't surprising that Joyce expected her to take care of the situation. She was used to being her go-to girl for everything in the office. She was her receptionist, secretary, and personal assistant, all in one.

"Actually, Joyce, that's a great idea. I've been telling you for ages that we need to overhaul our computer network and invest in an antivirus program."

"I know, I know. That's why I didn't hang up on the man. But Candace, you know I don't know a thing about computers. As long as it doesn't freeze up or melt down whenever I turn it on, I'm a happy camper." Picking up her purse and briefcase, she took her coffee and donut and escaped into her office, leaving Candace shaking her head.

• • •

"Dr. Jeffers's office, how may I help you?" The sultry timbre of the siren's voice filled Brice's ear, and he was mildly surprised that her effect on him was just as powerful over the phone. He held his breath for about three seconds, then plunged feet-first into unknown territory.

"Good morning. My name is Brice Coleman, and I represent the computer service company Security Matters. I spoke with Dr. Jeffers yesterday regarding an appointment to discuss our services. Is your specialist available sometime today, say, later this afternoon?"

"Good morning, Mr. Coleman. Dr. Jeffers said to expect your call, but I wasn't expecting it so soon."

"I'm sorry, I know it might make me seem a tad bit overzealous, but in my line of work one can't afford to let an opportunity get away. The competition is too stiff. I hope my eagerness doesn't count against me." Brice chuckled good-naturedly.

"Of course not. Can you hold while I check the calendar?"

"Sure. No problem." He was glad for the momentary silence. He needed a minute to gather his thoughts. Now that he'd made the call, he found himself second-guessing his decision. For a man who was methodical in everything he did, he had nothing that even remotely resembled a plan. He was going to show up under the pretense of giving a legitimate sales pitch, and wing it from there.

"Mr. Coleman?"

"Yep, still here."

"It looks like an hour or two can be freed up around two o'clock. How much time will you need?"

"I think an hour will be enough."

After a short pause she asked, "How does two-thirty sound?"

"It sounds perfect. Do you have a place I could set up for a one-on-one session?"

"I'm sure something can be arranged."

"All right, then. Two-thirty it is."

Chapter 7

Candace's eyes turned to the sound of the office door opening. She was taking a call when she looked up and stared into the impossible: the same aquamarine-blue eyes, black hair, and unforgettably handsome face she'd seen just two days ago. He was dressed in another Armani suit, and, like before, he looked as though he'd stepped out of the pages of a fashion magazine. Her heart stuttered and damn near skipped a beat. Never in her wildest fantasies did she expect to see that face again, or those eyes staring back at her. She cupped her hand over the phone's mouthpiece, glanced at the clock on the wall, and then back at the man in front of her.

"Mr. Coleman, I presume?"

"Right you are," he replied cheerfully. Candace nodded and held up a finger, indicating she'd only be a moment longer.

When the call ended, Brice said, "I know I'm early, but if the space we discussed is available, I can use the extra time to set up my equipment."

"It's okay. Actually, I was about to head over to unlock the door. If you'll follow me, I'll have you situated in no time."

Candace rose and led the way down an adjacent hallway until they reached a set of double doors. Unlocking them, she showed him inside.

"Would you like something to drink? Coffee, soda, or bottled water?"

"Water would be great."

"Okay, I'll be right back."

• • •

He stared at her backside as she walked away. His eyes soaked up the image of her broad shoulders, straight back, and luscious swaying hips, and burned it into his brain.

Brice selected a spot to set up and began arranging his equipment and materials. Still affected by her overpowering presence, he had a great deal of difficulty suppressing an enormous hard-on. He wasn't surprised. A stiff cock had been his constant companion for the last couple of days. Fortunately he'd have a small respite once he was introduced to the computer guy. He could push Candace's tantalizing form to the back of his mind, and pretend he had the situation under control. He'd deal with the problem of what to do next after the presentation.

Candace returned carrying two bottles of water and a pen and notepad—alone, without another soul in sight. She passed him a bottle, took a seat at the conference table, and looked up expectantly. He looked nervously at the closed door.

"Will your computer rep be joining us?"

"You're looking at her." Candace raised her brow and smirked at his look of surprise. "Look," she said, clasping her hands together on the table before her. "This is a small office with only a few employees. The title 'receptionist' doesn't begin to represent the true extent of my role within this practice. I have a master's degree in computer science, and I can assure you that I am well-versed in computer operations technology and security issues."

Brice was stunned. This was *not* what he'd expected.

"It was certainly presumptuous of me to assume that the rep would be someone other than the receptionist, but I am pleasantly surprised." He gave her a shaky smile, and nearly choked on the lie that spilled out of his mouth. *I am so screwed.*

"Now that that's cleared up, before you begin, I have a few questions." Candace picked up her pen and looked at her notepad, suddenly all business. "Tell me about your company. How long have you been in operation?"

"The name of the company is Security Matters, and we are an organizational software development enterprise. My partner and I only started the business over a year ago, but thanks to referrals and word-of-mouth, it has grown extensively. We've developed various multilevel antivirus software programs for businesses interested in streamlining their IT security planning and operations. Currently, our target audience is corporations with branches nationwide and internationally."

"Well, that sounds impressive, but I have to ask, if your main interest is in corporations and big businesses, why take small business referrals?"

Damn. Not even ten minutes into my spiel, and I'm already busted.

"That's a good question. A few days ago while I was giving a presentation, the subject of small businesses came up as a side discussion. Most small business owners know that cybercrime exists, but underestimate the severity of the threat and lack the training and technology to prevent it. Our client believed that corporations should develop programs to educate the smaller businesses, because what affects them could ultimately have a cascade effect on larger commercial enterprises. And I happen to agree with him.

"I told him that my company was interested in initiating a pilot program to educate and train the small business sector. I asked if he knew of any good candidates for what we had to offer."

There, that sounded plausible, didn't it? And for an idea that was generated completely off the cuff, it sounded good enough to actually consider putting into practice.

"Um, I guess that sounds plausible," she muttered, as if reading his mind. "What is your experience in the field?"

"I worked nine years as a computer programming specialist and software developer with another company, and I have a master's degree in computer science. Like you."

"Do you have a list of references?"

"Yes," Brice answered, and handed her a sheet of paper.

"So far, it sounds like an interesting process, driven by a logical purpose." Sitting back in her chair, she crossed her legs and gave him a heart-stopping smile. "Okay, Mr. Coleman, it's showtime. Impress me."

"Okay, but to tailor this briefing to suit your specific needs, can you tell me what problem areas you would like to focus on?"

"I'm concerned about the security of patient files and personally identifiable information, and how to address the threat beyond the traditional 'wall-and-fortress' approach. I'd like to know more about access to technical support and how often the operating system is updated with software patches. And I'd like easily accessible computer security awareness training for the employees."

Brice felt as though he'd been slapped in the face. She hadn't been kidding. Candace wasn't just a pretty face; she was technologically savvy and an honest-to-God computer geek. Suddenly he was caught up in the thrill of being with a woman who was sexy, beautiful, and the same freaking computer nerd that he was. Forgetting all about his anxieties and his hastily thrown together harebrained idea, Brice pulled out a chair and sat down next to her.

"Those are very valid concerns, Ms. Brown, and I'd be happy to address each one."

"Please, call me Candace," she interrupted, the sound of her voice softly tinkling in his ears, rolling over his scalp, and sliding down his spine. But this time he ignored the sensation, amazed at how much easier it was to do, now that he'd discovered there was more to her than just a pretty face.

"All right, then. Candace it is. And I'm Brice." Brice then segued into his presentation. They engaged in a back-and-forth discussion throughout his briefing, both excited about the prospect of applications, until his hour was finally up.

After putting away his equipment, he gave her handouts and company brochures along with his business proposal.

"You certainly get into your work, don't you, Brice?" Candace chuckled as his excitement winded down.

"Yes." He laughed. "I have to admit I get a certain kind of thrill from talking about computer techno stuff. It's my bread and butter and my second love."

"Second? What's your first?" She smiled openly and looked directly into his eyes.

"Music." He was standing too close, staring too deep, and falling too fast into those honey-colored eyes. "It gives me a kind of freedom." Now that the mental rush had dissipated, he quickly reverted back to feeling those incredible sensations he experienced each time he was near her. Candace returned his stare, her brows raised and her gaze inquisitive.

"So, Candace." He took a step back and made a concerted effort to break the threads of the spell she was weaving around him. "What do you think? Are we in bed together, or what?"

"Excuse me?"

"*Business.* Are we in business together?" he quickly amended, feeling a slow burning heat travel up the back of his neck and make its way to the tips of his ears. "Dr. Jeffers said if I sold you on my proposal, I could consider it a done deal. Are you sold?"

"Yep, I'm sold. It's a deal." She stood and offered her hand. He accepted.

Chapter 8

Brice sat in his usual spot on his oversized sofa, cradling his saxophone like a lover. Tonight, his mind was on Candace. The day's mission had failed miserably. In fact, it had made matters worse, because the more he'd learned about her, the more he was attracted to her. He'd walked away from his meeting more confused than when he'd started. Everything about that woman had him twisted into knots. *Not good.*

He rested his chin in his hand and thoughtfully considered the unopened bottle of tequila on the table. Normally he didn't much care for hard liquor. An ice-cold beer was his usual preferred poison. But tonight he might have to make an exception. Maybe a searing fire in his belly could make him forget the red-hot heat running through his veins. He got up and grabbed a shot glass, a knife and cutting board, a saltshaker, and a small bowl filled with limes. He returned to his seat and cut the limes into several wedges, and then broke the seal on the bottle and poured his first shot. The drink went down as smooth as silk, warming his innards as it streamed to his stomach, chased by salt and the biting tang of lime.

He picked up his saxophone again and leaned back into his position of meditation, his mind was blessedly blank. Then, out of nowhere, Homer's *The Iliad* and *The Odyssey* popped into his head, the two epic Greek tales of Ulysses's journey back to Greece after the Trojan War. The return route took the ship close to the Isle of the Sirens, mythical sea nymphs who possessed voices so irresistible they drove sailors mad and lured them to their death. Ulysses brilliantly saved the crew by filling their ears with melted wax. However, wanting to hear the voices for himself, Ulysses ordered his men to lash him to the mast of the ship. When the ship passed the Isle, the nymphs' voices were so compelling he fought and begged to be released. But fortunately, the wax prevented his men from hearing and obeying him, thereby saving his life.

It was no wonder Brice kept comparing Candace to a mythical siren. Everything about her reminded him of something out of a fantasy. With her looks, charm, and unbelievable voice, she could have stepped directly off the pages of a fairy tale. *All she needs is a pair of fluttering wings, a magic wand, and some fairy dust.* A chilling feeling traveled down his spine, and all of a sudden he felt a lot like Ulysses—fighting against his restraints and losing his grip on sanity. Leaning forward, he selected another lime and poured another shot.

• • •

He woke with a start, his eyes wide open and staring unblinking at the ceiling. His heart pounded hard as the lingering vestiges of a fantastical dream still swirled in his head. He lay in dazed silence, remembering the dream in shockingly vivid detail ...

They lounged upon a large blanket in a luscious green meadow under the low-hanging branches of a massive oak tree and picnicked on wine, fruit, and cheeses. Both were dressed in white, she in a long flowing pristine linen wrap, her arms, neck and shoulders exposed, and her feet bare. He wore linen drawstring pants and a matching loose-fitting shirt, completely unbuttoned. His chest and feet were bare. Her tawny brown hair, highlighted with streaks of strawberry blond, was springy and full of curls that spiraled around her face and fell about her shoulders. Looped around her neck was a long, wide chain of gold that held a large iridescent seashell amulet nestled between her breasts, and her ears were adorned with golden hoops. The warm rays of the sun shimmered radiantly on her soft, brown skin, and he lay there in the shade basking in the glow.

She fed him grapes, sunshine, laughter, and kisses, and he greedily took all that she offered. He could lie there forever with his head in her lap and her fingers running lightly, lovingly through his hair. They spent the day bathing in joy, whispering of love and wishing for forever after—until a sudden shift in the wind brought the smell of the ocean with the late evening breeze. His heart fluttered as he felt the harbinger of change that drifted in on the wind.

She stood and turned her head, listening to a voice only she could hear that seemed to come from the ocean beyond. He came to his knees and took her hand and placed it on his heart, to keep her with him a while longer. "No. Not yet," he begged. She smiled sadly and touched her fingers first to her lips then to his, then turned and ran across the meadow toward a stand of trees. Her white wrap flowed and billowed loosely in the breeze. She was a spirit in the wind.

He jumped up to follow, running through the trees to stop her. When he reached the end of the woods, he saw her standing at the edge of an overhanging cliff, facing the waters with her arms held high above her head. She looked like a high priestess. Her voice rose in song and went out across the waters to answer the call. The sound, melodic and magical, held him immobile, frozen in place. She spun and gave him one last look, then turned back to the ocean and jumped off the cliff's edge.

The spell broken, he ran forward to look over into the depths, to only see the white wrap floating on the incoming tide. He dropped to his knees, his face in his hands and his shoulders shuddering from grief and loss, until he heard a loud splash and the siren's musical voice once more. And there she was. Her beautiful hair had thickened and lengthened to cover her now-naked torso. Her arms were wrapped in golden bangles, and her necklace sparkled and glittered with the light of the setting sun. She cupped her hands to her mouth and sent a message on the wind, whispering that she loved him and that she'd see him again.

Then she was gone. The last thing he saw were the beautiful, iridescent blue-green scales of a very large fanned fishtail as it disappeared into the ocean ...

Brice stuffed his face into his pillow and groaned out loud. Too much alcohol and too much imagination equaled one hell of a dream. He rolled over flat on his back and stared up at the ceiling. He was stunned by the detailed memory of color, texture, and emotion—especially the emotion. It was so real he swore he could literally feel an ache in his chest.

"That's the last time I try to drink an entire bottle of tequila all by myself." He dragged himself out of bed and stumbled into the bathroom and was confronted by his reflection in the mirror. He saw sleep-tangled hair, the darkened shadow of a morning beard, and bloodshot eyes. He was still fully clothed. *What the hell happened last night?*

He stripped and got into the shower, hoping the hot water would clear the cobwebs. It helped, some. But his head hurt like hell. Afterward, he wrapped a towel around his waist and put on a pot of coffee.

The first sip of the hot liquid scalded his tongue and throat as it traveled down to his stomach. He didn't care that it hurt. The pain was penance for his stupidity. He took another sip, more cautiously now, and let the black gold warm him inside and ease the thumping in his head. He took his coffee and stumbled over to the breakfast nook and sat down. He lowered the cup with still shaking hands and turning his jumbled thoughts inward, he began to take silent inventory of his life.

At thirty-five, he was still single. It was by choice, not by fate. He enjoyed his life the way it was: free and uncomplicated. He wasn't afraid to settle down, but dammit, he wasn't ready yet. He'd watched as most of his friends took the plunge either into committed relationships or matrimony, David being the most recent to fall. So far he'd managed to sidestep the trap and keep his distance, but it seemed that everywhere he looked, love was in the air. *Like some kind of virus.* And he had a sinking feeling that he was about to be infected. Because no matter how hard he tried to fight it, he knew with every fiber of his being that Candace Brown was every bit the threat he'd first perceived.

Chapter 9

"Doctor Jeffers's office, how may I help you?"

"Hi, Candace, it's Brice. How are you doing today?"

"Hello, Brice. This is a surprise." There was a slightly puzzled note in her voice. "Isn't it customary to give a potential client a couple of days to review the proposal?" Her teasing lyrical lilt poured through his veins.

"Yeah, I know it's ridiculously early to be calling, but I guess I'm feeling a bit anxious. What did your boss think of my proposal?" He was stalling. For the first time in his life, he didn't know what to say to a woman.

"To be honest, I haven't brought it to her yet. She's been busy. But I promise I'll get with her today, even if I have to tie her to her chair."

"Yeah, okay. That's great, Candace." He paused and took a big breath. *Get to the point, you idiot, before you lose your nerve.* "But I think I should come clean about the real reason I called."

"There's another reason?"

"Yeah, there is. To be honest, I didn't call to ask about the proposal at all."

"You didn't?"

"No. I called to ask if you'd have dinner with me."

"Excuse me?"

"I'm inviting you to have dinner with me."

"Yes, I'm sorry. Of course you are." She sounded confused. "I heard you the first time. You just took me by surprise, that's all. Why are you asking me out to dinner? You don't even know me."

"That's why I'm asking you out. I want to get to know you." He contemplated all of ten seconds before making up his mind. He'd gone this far; he might as well take the plunge. "Look, Candace,

I'm going to be honest with you. I've been trying to avoid this very thing since the first time I saw you, and I don't mean yesterday. We both know we were in the same place at the same time four days ago. I was attracted to you then and it grew even more after our meeting. And, at the risk of blowing the possibility of your saying yes to my out of left field invitation, I may as well confess that I engineered the entire security meeting just to meet you face-to-face. *And* before you get the wrong idea, I'm not a stalker or a psycho, because believe me, I really tried to ignore the attraction. But I figured the best way to get you out of my system was to ask you out, and try to find something about you that I couldn't possibly like."

• • •

Although taken completely by surprise, Candace found his self-proclaimed predicament endearing and she couldn't help but interject a bit of humor into the moment. "I'm sorry to hear I've been the source of such irritation. I can't help but feel that I'm an innocent party in this, um, situation. However, I'd like to point out that we have a pending contract proposal between our two businesses. Now, in my mind, that presents a problem that falls somewhere between personal influence and professional ethics. For all I know, you may be trying to wine and dine me for the sake of a signature on a contract."

"No problem, I'll withdraw the proposal. Consider it null and void, and you can shred it."

"Wait a minute." She laughed. "I like the proposal, and my boss needs what you have to offer."

"Then make up your mind, woman," he teased. "What'll it be? Are you going to let a small thing like 'ethics' stand between doing the right thing and saving a man's reputation?"

"Reputation? What sort of reputation are we talking about?"

"I'll tell you all about it over dinner when you say yes."

"How about I let you know later? I need time to think this over."

"Sure, Candace, no problem. But to give you some peace of mind, we can meet anywhere you want, and I'll leave you with all my personal info. I don't want you to feel pressured or uncomfortable. I want you to feel safe."

She smiled at his thoughtfulness. She'd been on plenty of dates, but never with a guy who'd ever been so concerned about her state of mind. That alone was pushing the odds in his favor. "Okay, Brice, I'll take your invitation into consideration and get back to you later today." After taking down his personal information, they talked for a little while longer. He cracked jokes as he plead his case and had her laughing out loud.

She was still glowing over the call when Joyce arrived at the office.

"Good morning," Joyce delivered her normal cheerful greeting, then immediately became suspicious upon seeing the look on Candace's face. "Okay, spill it, right now. What's put that ear-to-ear grin on your face this early in the day? Because whatever it is, I want some of it."

"Oh Joyce, you'll never guess what happened," she said, excited. "But I think I need your advice."

"All right." Joyce quickly put her things down and came around to lean against the edge of her desk. "Ask away. I can't wait to hear what has you so giddy."

"Mr. Coleman called and asked me out to dinner." Candace recounted Brice's confession about how he'd engineered the whole affair, ending the story with a question in her eyes. "So, what do you think? Should I or shouldn't I?"

"He certainly is resourceful, I'll give him that. And at least he was honest enough to fess up. But I think that the real question is, do you *want* to go out with the man or not?"

"Yes. But I don't want to feel like it's a crazy thing to do. Considering he practically admitted to stalking me."

"Do you have his phone number?"

"Yes."

"Give it to me."

Candace warily handed over the number and watched Joyce punch it into the phone. Joyce was a consummate professional and an expert at handling tense circumstances, knowing exactly how to defuse a situation. But there were also times like now, when she could be brash and unpredictable. There was no telling what was about to come out of her mouth.

"May I speak with Mr. Brice Coleman, please? Mr. Coleman? Hi, this is Dr. Joyce Jeffers, Candace's boss. Yes, hello. I'm fine, thank you. No, I'm not calling about the proposal; it's about another matter entirely. Candace tells me you've asked her out on a date, but she has concerns, considering the circumstances behind your invitation. So here's what's going to happen. *I* will retain possession of your personal information. I will expect a call when she arrives for the date and another when it's over. I'm her backup plan, just in case you turn out to be some kind of psycho nut job who wines and dines and abducts his dates. If I do not hear from her at those designated intervals, I will call the authorities to report a kidnapping. And believe me, one call is all it will take. Do I make myself clear? Good. Now, here's Candace. You two can hash out the details. Enjoy your date."

Joyce grinned and winked at Candace as she handed over the phone and then picked up her things and went into her office, closing the door behind her.

Candace stared after Joyce in shock as she put the phone to her ear. "Brice. I'm so sorry. I had no idea she'd say those things. It's okay if you've changed your mind; I'll understand completely." To her surprise, on the other end of the phone was loud, irrepressible laughter.

"Wow," he said when he'd finally caught his breath. "That is one cool lady. I like her."

"You mean you're not upset?"

"Of course not. She's just looking out for you. I can't fault her for that. You're lucky to have someone who cares that much. Just give her everything she needs, and I'll be sure that you make those calls. I want to go out with you, Candace, but I don't want to end up in jail."

They made dinner plans for Saturday evening, and Brice was still chuckling when he said goodbye.

Chapter 10

They agreed to meet on Saturday evening at a popular restaurant in the downtown district. Brice made reservations for seven o'clock and was now standing in the lobby waiting impatiently for her arrival. He couldn't believe how anxious he was to see her again. When at last he saw her walking toward him, beautiful and serene, all the feelings of anxiety and impatience miraculously melted away. She smiled and held out her hand to greet him, which he raised to brush against his lips and then placed in the crook of his arm.

They followed the maître d' to a table in the middle of the large room and were seated amid the quiet din of laughter and conversation. The room was dimly lit with recessed lighting in the ceiling and along the walls, and flickering tea lights were placed inside crystal sconces on every table. Soft music playing quietly from an unknown source provided a romantic ambiance. When the waiter arrived, they ordered drinks and settled back to relax and enjoy the atmosphere.

"So, Brice, I'm dying to hear why you orchestrated such an elaborate scheme to find me. I'm flattered, but I can't imagine what it must have taken to pull it off, especially since we'd never even spoken to one another."

"It wasn't as difficult as you might think. After all, it's my business to know how people and corporations tick. I search for their vulnerabilities and exploit them in order to make them safe against an attack. I simply applied the same skills to find you. In other words, I lied my ass off."

She chuckled. "But why did you do it?"

"Because," he responded without hesitation, "I couldn't get you out of my head. You were a puzzle, and you presented a challenge with way too many questions. I needed answers." He paused and gave her a direct, meaningful look. "I need to know if you're as dangerous as I think you are."

"What does that mean?"

"It means," he said as he leaned forward and put his elbows on the table, "that I'd like to get to know you better. You fascinate me, Candace, and I'm not easily fascinated by women." Her eyebrows rose, and she crossed her arms and cocked her head to the side.

"I know that sounds a bit pompous," he chuckled and held his hand up, "but let me explain. What I mean is that my usual experience with women, from start to finish, is average. There are no sparks or fireworks. And I'm okay with that. I *like* average. It's safe. But I don't feel safe around you. Instead of tucking tail and running like I know I should, I want to know why."

"Well, you just put it all out there. No hesitation or beating around the bush. Don't you keep anything to yourself?" Her arms were still crossed.

"Sure I do. But as a rule, I don't like secrets. Secrets create drama, and I don't like drama. Life is complicated enough. I want to be honest with you, Candace. I don't know where this date is headed or if it will lead to something more, but I'd like to have all the facts before taking that next step."

Candace picked up her wine glass and gazed at the contents before lifting her eyes to meet his. "I appreciate your honesty and your methodical approach to the 'problem.' But I have to tell you I'm beginning to feel like some kind of science project or something. You're not the only one who'll be affected by this little experiment of yours, Brice. I'm a living, breathing person with thoughts and feelings. And contrary to your aversion to 'sparks and fireworks,' I thrive on them. For me, there's nothing more satisfying than the rush of dancing on the edge or playing with fire. Granted, the fireworks might explode in my face, but that's a chance I'm willing to take just for the adventure." She took a sip of wine and stared into his eyes.

Brice smiled. "That's precisely what fascinates me and makes me careful. I think you'd make me reckless and throw caution to the wind, and that would disrupt my otherwise well-ordered and meticulous life. I'm happy with my life as is." *I wish I were as sure now as I was four days ago.*

"So, is *this* the 'reputation' you alluded to? That's it? That you're a cautious, no-frills, no-fireworks kind of guy?"

"Yep, I'm afraid so. There are no deep dark secrets here; I'm just an average guy trying to maintain my average life."

"Yeah, right." She snorted into her glass. "I'll believe that when I see it. I think you should know, I Googled you, and there's nothing 'average' about you. You're all over social media, and your parents are high-profile too, with ties to the White House."

"That was a long time ago. My father retired from the embassy when the last president left office. He and my mother are tourists now, traveling to places they've never been, and returning to see others from a different perspective. As a matter of fact they're currently away on a yearlong trip to explore Europe, Asia, and South Africa. They'll probably spend most of their time volunteering, though. They're a couple of diehard activist types."

"That sounds exciting. Did you travel with them when you were younger? Do you have any siblings?"

"Yes, I did. And, no, I'm an only child. But I never really felt like an only child because wherever we lived, my mother practically adopted every kid in the neighborhood. She welcomed everyone into our home, especially other consulate members and their families. We Americans tend to stick together like family. You could say that I was practically raised abroad, because we didn't actually settle in the U.S. until I was in my late teens. Other than English, I speak three languages fluently."

"How did you end up here in Atlanta?"

"My mother is originally from here. She and my father met in college. He was a political science major and she was prelaw. They married young, and Dad worked for the Department of State and the Foreign Services for years, moving up the ranks. I was eight years old when Dad got his first foreign assignment as a consulate general."

"Wow. It must have been exciting growing up in so many different places. My dad traveled for his job a lot when I was young, but we never went with him."

"What did he do?"

"He was, and still is, a community investment consultant for global banking. Don't ask me what that means; I've never understood it. It has something to do with money and numbers and the global economy. I know enough to balance my checking account and pay my bills, and that's good enough for me."

He chuckled. "And your mom, what does she do? Do you have any brothers or sisters?"

"My parents met on the job. My mother was also working in the field of global banking and economy. So it was natural they'd hit it off. I'm sure you've already guessed that I'm biracial. My mother is Caucasian and my father is African American. So, I guess you could say," she gave him a slight smile, "I've grown up with my own version of cultural diversity."

Being the product of two different worlds, Candace had always been caught in between, never completely at home or accepted in either. She was too white to be black and too black to be white, and was never made to feel good enough for either race. No matter how self-assured and independent she was in nearly every aspect of her life, she still harbored deep-seated doubts about where she truly belonged. Even with changing views on interracial relationships and fewer raised eyebrows, in the end, ingrained traditions and beliefs often stifled the intrusive voice of diversity.

"Here's to cultural diversity, and may we continue to learn and explore whatever life has to offer." Brice, interrupting her thoughts, raised his glass for a toast.

"Here, here," she chimed in as she touched her glass to his. "And I have one older brother, whom I adore. He's my personal superhero and self-appointed protector."

She smiled inwardly at the thought. Her brother wasn't the only one who looked after her. Her entire family was overprotective. It didn't matter that she was nearly thirty years old; everyone still thought of her as the baby. But some things even her family couldn't protect her from, like her notoriously bad relationship decisions that often led to disastrous results.

• • •

They finished their meals, and as the waiter left to get their dessert order, Brice saw a familiar figure across the room. Blaine Stanford, an old friend he hadn't seen in at least eight months, was standing and talking with another man. Brice informed Candace about his friend and excitedly excused himself to go over and say hi. Blaine was the dictionary definition of tall, dark, and handsome, with dark, coffee-brown skin, gleaming white teeth, and short cropped hair. He was the perfect picture of success in his crisp dark-gray suit, black shirt, and tie.

"Blaine! Man, when did you get back in town? I haven't seen you in ages."

"Brice. Well if it isn't my blue-eyed soul brother." He chuckled in a deep baritone voice as they shook hands and briefly embraced. "I should have known I'd run into you since this place is so close to your stomping grounds. How are you? And where's David?" He gave a sweeping search of the room. "Aren't you two usually joined at the hip?"

"I'm here with a date." Brice gestured in the direction of where he'd left Candace.

"Um, I see you still have a sweet tooth for chocolate." Blaine's playful sarcasm was evident as he eyed Brice's date. "And I'll be damned if you don't always pick the choicest pieces from the box."

Brice grinned at his remark. The two of them had been friends for years, but it had taken Blaine time to accept that Brice's craving wasn't simply a matter of curiosity.

"Unfortunately for you, my friend, you've got more to worry about than me stealing from the candy dish. Our friend David has recently discovered his own love for rich dark chocolate. And he's hooked, but good. As a matter of fact, he's gone and swept his lady-love off on a tropical vacation for a few weeks. They wanted some private time together to get better acquainted."

Blaine gave Brice a startled and confused look. "What the hell are you talking about, man? First of all, David wouldn't let himself be tied down by *any* woman. And secondly, I know the type of women he's interested in—blonde, bony, and brainless. Are you telling me he got taken down by a sista?"

"That's exactly what I'm telling you. This woman has him so tied up in knots that it won't be long before she has him walking down the aisle."

"Damn. That's some serious shit. And speaking of serious," Blaine said as he looked over Brice's shoulder. "I think maybe you'd better get back to your table, man. It looks like someone is making a move on your woman, and she doesn't look too happy about it, either."

Brice turned to see a tall, lean man with shaggy light-brown hair leaning over Candace and invading her personal space. He was immaculately dressed and stood out with his light hair, pale white skin, and good looks. Candace was clearly upset.

"Yeah, I think you're right."

There was obviously history between them. The man leaned in close and rested one hand on the chair, deliberately brushing the other across her cheek and down her arm. His conduct showed a brazen lack of respect. "Excuse me, Blaine. We'll play catch-up later, but right now, I need to get back to my date."

Chapter 11

Candace watched Brice as he talked with his friend, loath to admit her fascination with this handsome and unusual man. He was actually a pretty nice guy, a far cry from what she normally scraped from the bottom of the barrel. She'd forgotten what it was like to date a decent man. *Which means this should probably be our only date.* She'd made an exception to her recent "no more dating" policy because, well hell, the man was too fine to say no. But though flattered by his admission of attraction and confusion, she didn't trust "nice." His dark good looks and polite behavior were charming, seductive—and hazardous to her health. Granted, she'd spent an inordinate amount of time undressing the man in her dreams, but dreams were much safer than rubbing up against flesh-and-blood reality.

He might appear cool and calm on the outside—leading the "well-ordered, meticulous life," he claimed—but there was something hidden well below the surface. Something raw and hot simmered beneath that deceptive layer of ice. It was difficult for the woman in her to resist the chance to explore. She wanted to unravel his meticulous world and start a fire that would make the Ice King melt.

She closed her eyes and tried to avoid those places her mind insisted on taking her. *Careful, Candy, you're letting your imagination run away with you again. It's just one date.* But, no matter how hard she tried to rein in her rampaging thoughts, it was a losing battle. That is, until she was interrupted by the light brush of warm flesh against her arm. She lifted her face to see Nash staring down with his characteristic smirk and almost unrecognizable menacing eyes. She was shocked and rendered speechless.

"What's wrong, Freak?" he taunted, leaning in closer. "You don't know who I am now?" Candace stared at him in silent disbelief.

"Who's the new guy?" he asked, inclining his head in Brice's direction. "If I didn't know better, I'd think you were trying to replace me." He boldly grazed her cheek with his finger and then let it slide down over her arm. "He looks too uptight and 'Dudley Do-Right' to me." He leaned forward and breathed in her ear. "It won't work, you know. I told you—this is the only place you can get your fix." He angrily spat the words and graphically grabbed his crotch to emphasize his point. "No one can handle that appetite of yours like I can. How do you think he'd feel if he knew just what kind of a freaky bitch he has on his hands? I bet he couldn't dump your ass fast enough."

Candace clutched the stem of her glass nearly to the point of snapping it in two. Her lips tightened into a thin line, and she glared defiantly into his eyes.

"You need to leave, Nash. You need to leave now," she hissed through clenched teeth. "I don't know what your problem is, but you should have gotten the message by now. Things are over between us. I suggest you take your self-centered, narcissistic, arrogant, *delusional* ass and leave. I know you have a highly over exaggerated opinion of yourself, so please let me be the first to inform you that you ain't all that."

• • •

Brice reached their table in time to hear that last statement. He gave the intruder an icy stare. "Is there a problem here?"

"No, not at all," the man responded indifferently. "Just saying hello to an old friend, that's all. Right, Candace?"

"Yes, and now we're saying good-bye."

"Now, Candace, don't give your friend here the wrong impression. We've had our differences, but we're still friends, aren't we? By the way," the man said, turning to offer Brice his hand, "my name is Andrew Nash, but folks just call me Nash."

"Brice Coleman," he responded coolly, ignoring the extended hand. As he regarded Nash's insincere smile and hard, flat eyes, a strong instant dislike settled in his gut. Yeah, there was history here, all right. He'd have to be blind or a fool not to see it. But he'd be damned if he'd back down from a confrontation with a former lover. He wasn't that easily intimidated.

Mutual dislike was apparent as they stood face-to-face, like two Roman gladiators about to do battle. Nash was the first to give ground when he spoke to Candace, his eyes never leaving Brice's face.

"I'll see you around, Candace. Give me a call sometime, and maybe we can get together." He nodded his head to Brice and walked toward the exit.

"When hell freezes over," she muttered, lifting her glass and emptying its contents.

Brice watched as Nash strode away. "A friend of yours?" he asked, turning his attention back to Candace.

"I'd hardly call him that." Her eyes were cast downward and stared into her empty glass. "More like an unfortunate mistake. We were lovers once upon a time, but we were never 'friends.'"

"How long ago was 'once upon a time,' if you don't mind me asking?"

"It ended months ago, but I don't think he's gotten the message yet."

"I have a feeling this guy doesn't think your message applies to him. He looks like trouble to me, Candace."

"You're probably right. But there's nothing I can do about it right now."

• • •

The more Brice learned about Candace, the more fascinated he became with the woman behind the voice. The evening had been a success, in spite of the unwelcome interruption by Andrew Nash. Now there was a man with some obvious issues. There was something overtly disturbing and sinister about him, and Brice didn't like the uneasy feeling he felt simmering in his gut. He had a feeling she hadn't heard the last of him.

Pushing nagging concerns aside about whatever unknown element Nash brought to the equation, Brice's thoughts returned to dwell on Candace. He considered calling her just to make sure she'd arrived home safely—and the thought surprised him. *Careful buddy, that's the first sign of getting sucked in.* But after only a few moments of hesitation, he ignored the warning and made the call anyway.

Chapter 12

On Monday morning, Candace looked up in surprise to see Joyce standing in front of her desk, hands on her hips and tapping her foot impatiently. "So? How did it go? I didn't grill you for details when you called after your date because it was late. But it's time to spill the goods. What was it like? Did you have fun? Was he nice? Is he a good kisser? Are you going to see him again?"

"Whoa, Nelly. Take a breath, okay?" Candace laughed. "I know it's been a while since we've dished about my love life because, well, I haven't had one. But it was just dinner."

"Humph. 'Dinner,' my ass. I saw the way he looked at you. I'd bet my Louis Vuitton luggage that his mind wasn't entirely on the menu."

"He was a perfect gentleman. So whatever you think he had in mind didn't happen. He kept his hands, his thoughts, and his lips to himself. Honestly, I had a nice time. Unfortunately, there *was* one snag in the evening—and he goes by the name of Andrew Nash. He showed up at the same restaurant."

"Um, that must have been awkward."

"Oh Joyce, you don't know the half of it. He was acting so strange, strange even for Nash. It was like he'd gone off the deep end or something."

"Why do you say that?"

"Because he's under some kind of illusion that we'll get back together, or that we've never broken up. I'm starting to wonder if I should be concerned about him."

Nash had changed. He wasn't acting like your regular garden-variety asshole anymore. All the signs said he was turning into something a lot more complicated. Before she'd come to her senses and dumped him, he'd made it perfectly clear that he couldn't have cared less about her, one way or the other. Now he was suddenly acting borderline certifiable? She could deal with ego and attitude. But craziness? That was a whole other ballgame.

Candace decided to tell Joyce about Nash's behavior since the breakup—including the phone call to the office. If anyone would know what to make of it, she would.

"I don't like the sound of this," Joyce said. "His behavior shows classic signs of being a stalker. Why didn't you tell me about this sooner?"

"I didn't think it was important. I thought he was just pissed because I ended the relationship. But after Saturday, I'm not sure what to think anymore."

"How did Brice react to the situation?"

"He seemed concerned. He thinks he's trouble."

"He may be right. Maybe I should have a chat with Brice. If Nash continues to harass you, you let us know. We'll figure something out."

"Hold up. Who's this 'we' you're talking about?" Candace laughed. "What makes you think Brice is still going to be around, or that he'd be willing to get involved with a woman with a potential stalker problem?"

"Oh please. I know pure primal attraction when I see it. And I can tell by the smile on your face that the feeling is mutual."

"Yes, well don't let appearances fool you—mine or his. I just got out of a 'primal attraction' relationship, and look where that's gotten me. Believe me, I'm in no hurry to trade one bad situation for more of the same."

She wasn't about to admit that she wanted to see more of Brice Coleman, despite her instincts and her inner voice. Yeah, she wanted to see "more" of Brice—*a completely naked and exposed Brice.*

"Do you honestly think that's what it would be like with him?" Joyce asked with quiet concern.

"No, not really. Brice is a man of a totally different caliber. He's considerate, open-minded, and not at all pushy. I think I like him, but he seems as cautious as I am about moving too fast. We're both just feeling our way and taking our time. We're planning to get together this weekend. He has tickets to a jazz concert *and* backstage passes."

"Color me surprised," Joyce said with teasing sarcasm.

Chapter 13

The week went by so slowly it seemed to take forever before Brice found himself standing at Candace's door with a bouquet of flowers in his hand.

Her eyes widened in surprise when she saw the small bunch of peach-colored roses mixed with green fern and delicate baby's breath. "Oh, Brice, thank you. How thoughtful and charming," she said as she buried her face in the petals and deeply inhaled their natural perfume.

"'Charming' is my middle name, but you can call me 'Prince' for short," he said with a chuckle.

"Prince Charming? Uh, I believe that name's already been taken. It'll take some powerful inducements to convince this girl you can live up to the reputation. But," she smiled while taking another whiff, "I must say, you're off to a good start."

"I'll have you know, I'm more than capable of rising to the task. I was trained at the hands of none other than Beatrice Coleman, my mother, the queen of etiquette and charm. She told me to never show up at a woman's door empty-handed. But, whatever I might lack in charm can be made up for in other ways."

"Really?" she asked with a naughty lilt to her voice as she reached out to take his hand. "I can't wait to hear more." She gave him an impish smile and guided him inside. "You can tell me all about it while I put these in a vase and finish getting ready."

· · ·

The plan was to have dinner first and then go to the concert. Brice was more excited than he let on, though still coming to terms with his growing attraction. Dinner was twice the fun and every bit as interesting as their previous date, and the concert was the icing on the cake. He was astonished to hear her singing along with the band. Discovering she was familiar with the music pleased him. Finally, when she threw her arms around his neck and sang the lyrics to him in her beautiful musical voice, he nearly melted in his seat. The woman was full of surprises.

After the concert he took her backstage to meet the band. Her eyes sparkled with excitement like she was a child on Christmas morning. He hadn't mentioned that the band members were personal friends and he'd sat in on jam sessions with them on numerous occasions. When she found out about his close connections, she looked at him with a kind of sweet and awed respect. And in that moment, he'd give anything in the world to have her look at him like that all the time.

• • •

"Thank you for a great evening, Brice. I had a wonderful time." Candace purposely took a step back to place distance between them. The scent of his cologne and the nearness of his body wreaked mayhem with her senses. The tantalizing, masculine smell of subtle spice aroused her desire, and her head filled with new fantasies and wild, improbable ideas. The combination of no sex in God knows how long and screaming hormones put her in the perfect position to make a Class-A fool of herself. Meanwhile, the answer to her prayers was staring her in the face. The man was entirely too sexy, too enticing, and too damn fine. If this date didn't end soon, she was going to do something stupid—*like climb all over him and jump his bones.*

She had every intention of ending the evening with her dignity intact and keeping her hands to herself. She leaned in to give him a sedate peck on his cheek and say goodnight, but unfortunately made the mistake of looking up into those glacial blue eyes.

She abruptly stopped short and found herself captivated by the intensity of his stare.

"You're not just saying that, are you?" He laughed lightly as he gently pulled her forward and tucked an unruly strand of hair behind her ear. The steady stare and the tender gesture froze her in place. She was drawn in by the desire and unconcealed raw passion she saw swirling beneath the surface.

"Of course not," she responded nervously, standing so close she could feel the heat from his body radiating between them. All of a sudden she felt vulnerable, unsure what to do with her hands. "Seeing how much you enjoyed being with your friends was the best part of the evening." She spoke quietly as her fingers brushed at imaginary lint and pulled timidly at the lapels of his suit. She looked up and allowed her eyes to travel over the strong features of his face. His lips drew her focus and dragged her inexplicably forward, like two strong magnets pulling her in against her will.

Her heart pounded in her chest and thundered in her ears as she stared in near-breathless expectation. He leaned down and lightly brushed her lips, and her hands firmly gripped his lapels and pulled him forward the rest of the way. Their lips met with tentative and tender exploration, testing the softness and feeling the hunger that surged and arced between them. He tasted of wine, after-dinner mints, and the promise of blistering-hot, toe-curling sex. She pulled him closer and held on tighter as the kiss deepened and became more potent.

He held her face in his hands as he plunged his tongue into the heated depths of her mouth, stroking her tongue and teasing her inner recesses. Freeing her face, he cupped the back of her head with one hand as the other crept lower to palm her bottom and pull her in flush against his growing arousal. There was no mistaking his attributes or his desire. *Just like in my fantasy*, she thought vaguely as reticence and resistance merged and melted away. She eagerly pressed forward, forgetting all her good intentions, lost in the heat of his kiss and the stirring sensation of his hardening manhood pushed intimately against her. The kiss was charged with electricity that infused her veins and short-circuited her brain, and neither could stop the powerful rush of energy that filled the air and crackled and snapped around them.

They were a jumbled mess of lips, arms, and legs in a matter of seconds. It seemed to go on forever, an unending exchange of breath, passion, and raw desire, curling her toes and sending bursts of scorching heat straight to her already aching core. Enveloped in a spiraling vortex of flames, she was unaware and uncaring that there was no chance of escaping being singed by the blaze. Eventually, the need to breathe prevailed. She gradually became aware of her breasts pressed flat against his chest and her back against the wall. She reluctantly surfaced and recovered enough of her senses to draw back from the edge of no return.

This had to stop, now, before they ended up stripped naked on her front doorstep. On some deep-rooted level of self-preservation, she knew instinctively that sex with Brice could mean trouble down the road. He wasn't anything like the type of men she usually dated, a warning in itself she could be dealing with elements beyond her control. The thought was enough to force her to pull away, and once again put distance between them. Taking a much-needed breath, she made herself look him squarely in his artic-blue eyes, fierce with unappeased hungry desire.

"Brice. We have to stop." She pressed shaky hands upon his chest as her mind struggled desperately to reclaim her lost wits. "I'm sorry. I'm not a tease. Really, I'm not. But, right now, I'm experiencing a little confusion. My body's saying one thing, and my head is saying something else. There's no way I can possibly deny how turned on I am, and I won't even try. But I'm not ready to let the heat of the moment overrule good sense." *Not yet*, she thought, giving a nervous laugh.

Brice gave her a brooding look and brushed his thumb across her lower lip before he reluctantly released his hold and stepped back. He stuck one hand in his pocket and scrubbed the other down his face. Shaken and confused, he appeared to be filled with the same warring feelings and doubts.

"It's okay, Candace. I'm a big boy. I can take no for an answer," he responded hoarsely. "Just—just give me a minute. I need a moment to readjust my thinking." He took a steadying breath and backed up a little further. "I think you're right. We should slow down. There's no need to rush into something we may both regret later, after the sparks have died out. Let's just call it a night. Besides, we have all the time in the world to get to know each other."

He reached out and gave her upturned face one last gentle brush with the back of his hand, then moved aside to allow her to unlock the door. She pressed the key to the lock, when unexpectedly the door cracked and swung inward. Brice immediately reached out and pulled her back and away from the open door. Candace's eyes grew wide in alarm.

"This can't be. I know I locked it when we left."

"Yeah, I know you did." Brice pulled her away from the house, back toward his car. "Does anyone else have a key?" he asked.

"No, no one except Joyce."

He took out his phone and called 911.

• • •

"I don't want to stay here," she whispered, her voice trembling. "He might come back. I don't want to be here alone." Candace and Brice stood in the middle of her living room staring in disbelief. The place was in ruins, vandalized. Scattered about the living room were shattered picture frames; family photos had been removed and torn to shreds. Books had been pulled from shelves, pages torn and bindings broken, and thrown into a pile on the floor. In the bedroom, her clothes had been pulled from the closet and thrown about onto the bed, the chair, or the floor. The room looked as though it had been hit by a tornado. Her underwear had been taken out of the drawers and ripped to pieces and thrown onto the floor as well. Written in lipstick on the mirror above her dresser was the word WHORE. The entire place looked as if it had been ransacked by an angry mob.

"Do you have somewhere you can go, Candace? Friends, family? Can you stay with Joyce?"

"Joyce left town for a seminar two days ago. My other close friend is out of town, too. I can't go to my parents' house. I don't want to worry them. They'd freak out and use this as an excuse to insist I move back home."

To see Candace this frightened and confused was heart-wrenching. The proud, confident woman he'd come to know and admire was suddenly vulnerable and unsure. A fierce sense of protection suddenly prompted him to pull her into his arms and hold her against his chest. "Get your things. You're coming with me. We'll call Joyce, tell her what happened, and let her know where you'll be."

"What do you mean? Where are we going?"

"I'm taking you home with me for the next few days, until we can sort things out. I have three extra bedrooms and plenty of space. We'll let the police take it from here. Now go. Put some things together. But, if you'd rather, I'll take you to a hotel. Whatever you want, Candace. Just tell me, and I'll take care of it."

"Why would you do that? This isn't your problem." Her voice was low and on the verge of tears.

"You're right, it's not, but I'm making it my problem. I won't stand by and let you deal with this alone." He gave her a gentle push. "Pack enough stuff for a couple of days. I'll call Joyce."

Candace went to do as Brice urged as he pulled out his phone.

"Hello, Joyce? This is Brice."

"Hi, Brice. This is a surprise."

"Yeah, I know. Look, there's been an incident. Someone broke into Candace's townhouse while we were at the concert."

"What?! Where is she? Is she all right?"

"Candace is fine. She was with me when it happened, but she's definitely shaken up."

"What happened?"

"Her place was trashed. The police have already come and gone. They took photos and whatever information we could provide during their preliminary investigation. The door doesn't have much damage, but inside the place is a mess. I think I know who did it."

"You don't think it was Nash, do you?" she asked quietly.

"Yeah, that's exactly what I think. This wasn't random. It was personal—the torn photos and the ripped underwear, and especially the vulgar message left on the mirror. You and I both know the guy has all the makings of a certifiable nut job. I'm going to take her home with me. We just wanted to keep you updated."

"Thank God you were there. I'll be back on Tuesday. Can I speak to her?"

"Sure." Brice found Candace standing in the middle of the mess in her bedroom, wringing her hands and staring at the message on the mirror. His heart twisted again at the sight, and his jaw stiffened with resolve. He would find Andrew Nash and personally kick his ass.

Chapter 14

Forty minutes later, they walked through the front door of Brice's home. Candace had remained silent during the entire trip, in shock and staring out the window. Brice had held her hand, offering up reassurance and support. She stood in the vestibule and waited as he locked the door behind them. Brice took her hand and her bag and led the way into the heart of the house, the family room and the kitchen. When she saw the spacious room, comfy furniture, and huge in-home theater and surround-sound equipment, her eyes grew wide and her mouth dropped open. She turned to him in awed admiration and said, "You have nice toys."

Brice chuckled. "Yeah, it's your typical man cave. Sometimes I get lost in here for days at a time. Let me show you the rest of the house." He gave her a quick tour of the lower level, which included an office that doubled as a music studio, the guest bathroom, the laundry room, and the master suite. "The other bedrooms are upstairs. You can have your pick."

When she'd seen each room, she settled on the second master suite. It had large, masculine pieces of furniture and a king-sized sleigh bed with lots of pillows and a heavy comforter. She was instantly tempted to sink down into that huge bed and let all her troubles disappear among the pillows and plush covers.

"Everything you need should be right here," he said as he showed her the bathroom and the linen closet. "Take your time getting settled. I'm going downstairs to make us a couple of drinks."

She joined him downstairs in the family room a few minutes later. "This is a really nice place, Brice," she commented.

"Thanks. I like it." He handed her a cocktail. "I didn't know what you preferred, so I took the liberty of making you one of those fruity drinks." He smiled as he handed her the glass. "It's an apple martini."

"Thank you. I like apple martinis." She took the drink and downed most of it in a couple of gulps.

"Do you think it could have been Nash?" he asked. "Given his recent behavior, it wouldn't be a far stretch to consider him a suspect."

"Nash? Why would you think it was Nash?" she blurted out, surprised. "He doesn't even live here in Atlanta. He lives in New York City. I only saw him once or twice a month, when he came here on business. He's never even been to my house. Besides, why would he do something like this? I know he's been acting strange, but he wouldn't go that far. Would he?" Fear and confusion flooded her. It hadn't occurred to her that this might have been a personal attack.

She must have looked distressed, because Brice dropped his line of questioning. "You're probably right. I guess I'm blaming the guy because I don't like him. Let's just forget it. You don't have to think about any of this right now, and you're welcome to stay here for as long as you want to."

"Thank you, Brice, but I don't want to impose any more than I already have. I'll stay tonight, but tomorrow I should probably go to a hotel. I know I can't go back home yet. I need time to clear my head and figure out what to do next."

"Look, Candace, you're not disrupting anything. I wouldn't have offered if I didn't want to help."

"You really are a sweet man," she said. She reached up to cup his cheek in her hand and planted a soft kiss on his lips. "Thank you for everything. If you hadn't been there, I don't know what I would have done." She stared up at him, her eyes brimming with unshed tears.

He gently pulled her close and wrapped his arms around her. Pressing her face against his throat, he rested his chin on her head.

"Don't worry, Candace. I'll fix this. I'm not letting him get away with this, whoever he is."

"Are you going to be my knight in shining armor?" she whispered, her voice muffled, as she snuggled closer.

"I will if you let me."

• • •

Brice rubbed his hands gently up and down her back. Sighing deeply, Candace shook her head and pushed back from his embrace, obviously weary and still shaken up.

"If you don't mind, I think I'll take a shower and go to bed now. I'm kind of tired."

"Sure, a shower and a good night's sleep will be good for you." He reluctantly released her, and she climbed the stairs out of sight. "Let me know if you need anything else," he called after her. His heart pounded in his chest, beating hard in response to the feel of her soft lips, the warmth of her body, the smell of her perfume—and the growing need to shield her from all the world's unexpected cruelties.

He closed his eyes. A flood of emotions tore through him like a runaway train: his desire for her body, the fading willpower to resist her allure, and his overwhelming need to watch over and protect her. The depth of the unfamiliar feelings concerned him, but he'd deal with that later. Right now there was something else he had to do, something much more pressing.

Brice fixed another drink and went into his office and closed the door behind him. Since the room doubled as his studio, it was also soundproof, and that was a good thing. He needed absolute privacy for what he was about to do. He rummaged through his desk until he found what he was looking for, then picked up the phone and made a call to his private investigator, Richard Thorne.

Thorne, former Special Operations Forces with the Marines, had once been the Agent in Charge assigned to his dad's personal protection detail. Having worked primarily in hostile foreign environments, he was a trained counterterrorism, weapons, and self-defense expert. Richard Ashton Thorne was the living, breathing badass you only read about in books or saw in movies, the stuff heroes were made of. He'd successfully taken his military experience and crossed over into the civilian sector, and now ran a highly sought after PI and personal security consultant firm.

Brice had used his services on numerous occasions to breach company security of potential clients and, when necessary, for other, more personal reasons. Being the son of a former high-profile political figure and a wealthy man in his own right, Brice often had need of Rick's expertise. Personal security had been drilled into him since childhood, so he never took anything or anyone at face value. When he needed something checked out, he called Rick.

Thorne had access to unique state-of-the-art super gadgets and high-tech information databases. He was the consummate professional, a man of few words who got results.

Brice couldn't shake the feeling that Nash was responsible for trashing Candace's place, and Rick Thorne was just the man to find out if his gut intuition was right.

"Rick, this is Brice. I've got a job for you."

"Sure. What's the target?"

"It's a special job."

"Special jobs come with special prices."

"I know. That's not a problem."

"What's the name?"

"Andrew Nash. I don't know much about him except that he lives in New York City and travels here to Atlanta for business once or twice a month. There's no evidence to prove it yet, but I believe he broke into and vandalized my friend's home. I want him investigated, and if he's the threat I think he is, then I want the problem dealt with, or eliminated.

"I want to know his every move for the past month: phone calls, contacts, business trips, et cetera. I want to know where he works, where he lives, and what kind of car he drives. I want to know every detail there is to know, because when I'm done with him, I want to make sure he'll never threaten another living soul." Brice gave a brief description to get the investigation underway.

"Okay. What's the deadline?"

"How about yesterday?"

"I'm on it. I'll have a preliminary report in a few days."

"Good. I look forward to hearing it."

Brice made a couple more calls, one to his security service and one to a locksmith. He gave them instructions to replace all the locks at Candace's house and to drop the new keys off the next day. The police had temporarily secured her place, but something more permanent was needed. He knew he was overstepping his boundaries, but he didn't care. He'd deal with the consequences tomorrow. Having accomplished everything he could for the moment, Brice showered. After putting on pajama bottoms and an undershirt, he decided to make one last check on Candace before going to bed. When he reached her door, he found it ajar. Peeking inside, he overheard quiet sniffles.

"Candace? Are you okay?"

"Yes," was the muffled response that came from beneath the bedcovers.

"May I come in?"

"Yes."

Brice went to the edge of the bed and eased down beside her, putting his hand on her back. To his surprise, she abruptly turned and wrapped her arms around his waist and buried her face in his chest, sobbing quietly. The sight of tears in her eyes moved him and melted something deep inside.

He was a take-charge kind of guy. If someone was in need, he dove right in—up to his neck if need be—without hesitation. He made decisions quickly, with no fears and no regrets. That's what he did. That's who he was. Emotion had no part in his decision-making process; it was a distraction that he couldn't afford. Up until now, he'd made it a point to stay away from women with whom he might share strong common interests. He didn't want to see them as individuals with personalities because that made them more human, and it made him more vulnerable. But there was something about *her* tears that twisted his stomach and jolted his heart.

He stretched out beside her and pulled her fully into his embrace. Holding her to him, he kissed her eyelids and tasted her tears. "Shh, baby, don't cry. Everything's going to be okay. I promise." His kisses were deliberately soft and tender as he pressed his lips to her tear-streaked face. His mouth moved down the curve of her upturned cheek and lightly brushed across her pouted lips. The moist and silky softness he encountered triggered his natural male instinct, and pushed him beyond his ability to resist.

This is a mistake.

His mouth settled over hers, and she tentatively opened to allow him entry. He was swept up in a whirling pool of sensual heat that pulled him in deeper under her spell. What had begun as a show of support was fast becoming something more meaningful.

She shifted her body and pressed closer and held on tighter. He took the kiss deeper. The hardened tips of her breasts pushed into his chest and brought chills to his body, raising goose bumps that prickled his flesh. She moved against him in slow, sensuous, grinding circles, and the chill became a spark that ignited and burned into passion. Hunger raced through his body, fed by the warmth of her touch. Rippling sensations flowed through his core as bursts of fiery desire reached every part of him, from the base of his scalp, down to his toes.

He sought out the sweetness of her mouth and descended further into its softness. His body responded, and his cock hardened and lengthened, destroying any vestige of doubt that he craved this woman.

But with supreme effort, he pulled back from the edge of insanity. No matter how badly he wanted her, he wouldn't allow the situation to push either of them too quickly into something they might regret. He reluctantly ended the kiss, and, resting his forehead against hers, he drew in a ragged breath.

"Candace, honey, I didn't come up here for this. I came up to make sure you were okay."

"I know." She whispered and reluctantly loosened her hold. "I'm sorry. I didn't mean to molest you." She gave a small, tremulous laugh. "It's just that it's been so long since I've been held like this. It feels good. With everything that's happened, I think tonight more than anything, I needed to feel good."

"It's okay. Anytime you need to be held, just let me know. I'm your man for the job." He chuckled softly as he wrapped his arms around her again. "And just ignore *him*," he said, referring to his apparent arousal. "He has a mind of his own. I don't intend to take advantage of you while you're in this state. *When* we make love," he said, lifting her chin and looking into her eyes with unwavering certainty, "it won't be because you need a distraction. Call me old-fashioned, but when it happens, I want both of us fully engaged."

She rewarded him with a small smile. "Will you stay with me for a while, at least until I fall asleep?"

"Of course."

She kissed him on the lips again and then turned over on her side. Snuggling deeper into his arms, she pushed her bottom up flush against his arousal and gave a quick little wiggle.

"Stop that," he admonished, laughing in her ear. "I'm trying to be the bigger person here."

"Oh, there's no question you're the 'bigger' person." She giggled into the pillow. He purposely groaned out loud, making her laugh harder.

He was glad she was feeling better, even at his expense. Her laughter reassured him she had bounced back and put aside her fear, at least for the moment. The feel of her body, warm and soft cradled next to his, and her fresh-from-the-shower scent made him realize he couldn't have left her bed even if he'd wanted to.

He ended up staying the entire night with his body wrapped intimately around her, feeling an unfamiliar but welcome sense of warmth and satisfaction. He slept comfortably with his arms around her and his erection nestled against the cleft of her buttocks. To his surprise, he adjusted quickly to her restless movements in the night and the light sound of her snoring. Whenever she moved, he instinctively tightened his hold and snuggled closer, nuzzling her neck and shoulder, and folding himself more protectively around her.

Chapter 15

At the first sign of morning light, Candace stirred and came fully awake to the pleasant sensation of a warm body lying beside her, and strong masculine arms surrounding her. Smiling with the pleasant memory of where she was, she rolled over see beautiful sleepy blue eyes peering at her from beneath a cap of dark and tousled hair.

"Good morning." She reached up to brush aside wayward strands that threatened to obscure his sight. "What beautiful blue eyes you have," she said as she wrapped her arms around his neck and kissed him on his chin.

"The better to see you with," he growled playfully.

Nuzzling in closer, she was again made painfully aware of his arousal pressed intimately against her thighs. "Um, now that the three of us are awake, what *ever* should we do?"

"I told you to ignore him. He has a one-track mind. Besides, he always wakes up long before I do."

"You know," she said, pinning him with a meaningful look, "eventually we're going to have to do something about his shameless behavior, right?"

"I'm counting on it. But it won't be today."

"Well, if you insist." She pouted. "I suppose I'll let you get away with this sweet, albeit misguided attempt at chivalry for now. But you should know up front I'm a high-maintenance kind of girl used to having her way. So, consider yourself forewarned. Right now, I'll settle for being fed. What's for breakfast?"

"Are you going to be this demanding the entire time we're together?"

"Absolutely." She grinned.

He grinned back and kissed her on her nose, and then untangled himself from her arms and quickly got out of bed. "If you're going to stay here, you'll have to pull your weight. Meet me in the kitchen in ten minutes." He turned and left the room.

Candace lay in bed a while longer. She hadn't been the least bit alarmed by Brice's earlier statement that they would make love. The attraction was mutual, and the two of them becoming intimate was inevitable. She'd enjoyed lying next to him all through the night and had felt safe cuddled in his arms—a feeling she was woefully unaccustomed to.

Poignant memories of nights with Nash, void of intimacy and affection, flashed in her head. *Nash? Crap. Where did he come from to ruin my feel-good moment?* She didn't want to think about him right now—who he really was or what he might be capable of. She was with Brice, and Brice was nothing like Nash. That thought put the smile back on her face and made her jump out of bed and hurry to the bathroom. She quickly washed her face, brushed her teeth, and combed her wild, curly mane of hair up into a bushy ponytail perched on the top of her head.

Still dressed in cotton drawstring pajamas and a tank top, she hurried downstairs to meet Brice in the kitchen. What she saw there stopped her dead in her tracks, tightened her nipples, and sent a flash of warmth straight to her center, causing it to ache and throb with anticipation. Brice was bent over in front of the refrigerator, his muscular arms flexing as he reached inside. His firm rear end was so enticing it took every ounce of self-control she had not to walk up behind him, grab his ass, and rub all over him like a cat in heat.

The man had a body to die for: tall and lean with well-defined abdominals and chest muscles beneath an undershirt that stretched tight across his torso. His arms were muscled and roped with veins that stood out with implied strength. He was virtually a walking advertisement for a gym membership, and he'd be perfectly cast in one of those TV infomercials selling newfangled workout equipment. She knew he looked good in a suit and tie, but hot damn, he looked even better dressed in less. When he'd come to her room under the cover of darkness, Lord knows she'd felt every hardened inch of him pressed against her, separated only by two thin layers of cloth. Now in the light of day, she ogled his near-naked glory, feeling damp and needy—and wishing like hell he weren't so determined to be a gentleman.

Of course, he picked that instant to stand up and catch her gawking. Her eyes were immediately drawn to the impressive outline of his "friend," which she'd enjoyed pushing tight and aroused against her all night long. The full frontal was even more magnificent as it hung low and swayed from side to side. She had to lean against the counter to keep from collapsing on the floor. The unexpected rush of heat and desire made her dizzy. *Oh my God. He's got a six-pack—and packing an extra nine down below.*

"Caught you looking." He grinned as he closed the refrigerator door with his hip, his hands full of food for breakfast.

"Damn right you did," she said defiantly, clinching her fists as a rosy blush spread across her face and down her throat. "Traipsing around the kitchen wearing fancy pajamas and precious little else, you're lucky that 'looking' is all I was doing."

Brice laughed out loud. "I apologize for the distraction, but this is the most I've worn in my own home in years. So, *you're* lucky I'm not 'traipsing' around in my birthday suit."

Lord o' mercy. I did not need that visual running through my head. "Then I'll overlook your exhibitionism, this time," she countered flippantly with her nose in the air. "But a girl can handle only so much testosterone in an enclosed space. So don't blame me if I look at you like a dog drooling over his favorite toy. If you insist on making such a blatant display, then you have no one to fault but yourself."

"Okay," he chuckled. "Let's put you to work. You said you were hungry, so we need to get you fed." He gave her a mischievous look and wiggled his eyebrows. "Maybe a full stomach will help take the edge off?"

A full stomach is not what I had in mind. She felt a more ferocious hunger taking hold. She stood aside as he placed breakfast food and cooking utensils on the counter. From the looks of it, he was preparing to feed an army, with fruit, eggs, bacon, sausage, and fixings for pancakes.

"What can I do to help?"

"How good are you with a knife?"

• • •

"What are we going to do today?" she asked around a mouth full of bacon and pancakes. She sat with one leg tucked under her body and the other foot in the chair with her shin pressed against the table. They'd prepared their meal together like a well-organized team, talking and joking the whole time. He'd enjoyed the way she chattered on and on, telling funny stories from her childhood that made him laugh out loud.

He loved listening to her. Her face was freshly scrubbed, and she wore no makeup. The polished, professional woman he knew her to be had vanished for the moment, but he found himself liking this casual side of her even more. He'd been astonished by her admission of voyeurism and lustful yearning, delivered in a sullen tone. Hearing a woman unapologetically admit to her carnal desires was a new experience. And he liked it.

He was amazed at how comfortable he felt with her his home, and even more amazed that he hadn't panicked at the thought. It was a pure delight to have her in his kitchen and to watch her eat. He was experiencing a lot of "firsts" with Candace. It was the first time he'd invited a woman into his home to stay for more than a night. It was the first time he'd spent the night in bed with a woman and had actually slept. And it was the first time he'd ever played the role of that knight in shining armor, to rescue the damsel in distress. She'd brought out protective instincts in him he didn't even know he had.

"It's Saturday, so there's not much going on, but I've got a few errands to run. You can tag along if you like, or you can stay here and take it easy."

"Your offer sounds tempting, Brice." She emitted a small sigh, brushing her hands together to rid them of the last few bits of clinging crumbs. "But I should get back to reality and decide what to do about my problem. You've made me all but forget that my house was broken into last night. I'm grateful for the distraction, but I should go home and check on things." A wry expression settled on her face. "I should at least have the locks changed, and probably shop around for better security. Could you drop me off before you run your errands?"

"It's already been taken care of. Your locks are probably being changed as we speak, and someone should drop your new keys off sometime today. You can call around for a new security service from here. I happen to know of a couple of good companies I could recommend." He poured another cup of coffee and calmly awaited her reaction to the news. But it didn't matter what she said, he'd already made up his mind between bed and breakfast. There was no way he'd let her out of his sight, today or tomorrow. He wasn't about to leave her to deal with her problem all alone. And if he could stretch their time together into next week, well, he'd do that too.

"What? What are you talking about?"

"I called a locksmith last night, and I had security guards posted in front of your place until he got there."

Her eyes grew wide with surprise. "You did what?"

Brice sighed and carefully placed his coffee cup on the table. "Look, Candace, I told you I'd take care of things, so I did. And if you don't want to go home right away, you don't have to. You can stay here for the weekend, or until you're ready to face your place again. However long it takes. So, you can hang out with me for the day while I take care of some personal things. And then later, we can go out to dinner to the fanciest restaurant in town."

"I didn't bring anything to wear to the 'fanciest restaurant in town.'"

"We can go shopping. I'll buy you whatever you think you'll need for the evening."

"You're taking this 'knight in shining armor' thing a little too seriously, aren't you?" she commented with knitted brows and wary eyes.

He ignored her brief look of distrust. He didn't blame her, given what she'd gone through in the last twenty-four hours and her past experiences with Nash. Of course she had reservations, but he'd make damn sure she'd come to know that *he* wasn't Andrew Nash.

"Don't worry, Candace, I'm beginning to like the role. Humor me. It's not often I get a chance to play the good guy. And," he added with a grin, "I'm going to milk it for all its worth. So, what do you say? It's your call." He reached over to gently brush crumbs from the side of her mouth and gave her a penetrating look he knew she'd be unable to resist.

"That's not fair," she grumbled. "How am I supposed to say no to those eyes?"

"You're not supposed to say no. You're supposed to say yes."

• • •

They spent the morning together running his errands. Afterwards they had lunch and then stopped by Candace's house to check on the locksmith. He felt it was too soon for her to face the destruction again, but she'd insisted, wanting to see the damage in the light of day. The woman had a stubborn streak the size of Texas, and though he'd rather not admit it, he found it adorable. She also refused his offer to buy her something new to wear for their dinner date. She maintained she had a closet full of clothes and could certainly salvage something from the mess. They'd arrived at her house in time to meet with the locksmith and pick up the new set of keys.

When they went inside, she got upset all over again, but her reaction was far different from that of the night before. Instead of being frightened and confused, she felt angry and violated. Brice was right; she wasn't ready to deal with this yet. She needed more time. She was lucky she had a place to go to distance her from the problem. She trusted him enough to take advantage of the refuge he offered. She gathered together a few extra things to take back to his place, and they left.

Chapter 16

"I hope you don't mind this last stop before dinner. I promised my parents I'd look in on their place while they're away. It won't take but a minute." Brice's parents owned a penthouse above the high-rise hotel residences of the St. Regis Atlanta Hotel. Each residence featured expansive, open spaces with high ceilings, private outdoor terraces, and breathtaking views of the city.

The two entered the private lift that would take them to the top floor.

"Of course I don't mind. Besides, this is nice. I've never been inside a private elevator before. I'm impressed."

"Good. Then my plan is working."

"What plan is that?"

"To blatantly entice you with extravagant material trappings, of course." Brice leaned against the side of the elevator with a slight smile on his face and both hands stuffed deep inside his pockets. "The idea is to distract you with shiny trinkets and pretty baubles to keep you from looking too closely at the man. Otherwise," he reached out to tuck that one stubborn and unruly curl back in place behind her ear, "you might see all his faults and find him sorely lacking."

Candace smiled up at him, leaned in close, and draped her arms around his neck, pressing her body flush against him.

"I've got news for you. It's too late," she murmured under her breath as she sensuously moved against him, no longer able to resist the intoxicating pull of his erotic scent. "I've already seen your flaws. The only 'pretty bauble' I'm interested in at the moment is the tall blue-eyed Ice King standing in front of me."

So far, she'd been a good girl. She'd kept her distance. She'd held up her end of the conversation and laughed at the appropriate moments, all while looking but not touching. She'd tried her darnedest to ignore those broad shoulders, rippling muscles, and flat abs hidden beneath his shirt, and that impressive bulge in his pants. But standing together in this tiny space filled with the smell of his cologne, was asking too much of a hot blooded sexually frustrated woman. The memory of his hard length pressed tight against her bottom made her body tingle with desire and her thighs spasm. The crackling undercurrents that sparked from being too close to a live wire made her positively weak in the knees.

It was a waste of precious time to fight the urge, and she was done with trying. She simply had to wrap her body around his, caress him with her hands, and put her mouth on him. *I just need a taste, that's all. I'm sure a taste will be enough.* The elevator slowed and eased to a gentle stop on the floor of his parents' residence. The doors opened momentarily, and then silently glided shut.

She tugged his face toward her pursed lips and lightly pressed a string of kisses along his cheek. Savoring his scent in her nose and the taste of him on her lips, she adjusted her hold as her lips traveled the curve of his jaw on a journey to his mouth. With her fingers tangled in his hair, she stroked the back of his neck and urged him forward toward her skimming lips.

He opened his mouth and allowed her tongue to sweep inside. She searched, tasted, and thrust deep, stroking the roof of his mouth and his tongue. Now with her feet set solid onto the path, there'd be no stopping.

She reached her arms inside his suit coat to encircle his body and press closer into his heat. Her hands slid down his back, flowed over every muscle, traced every ridge, and tingled with each discovery. She paused for a moment, her heart beating wildly, waiting to be admonished for her bold behavior. When no reprimand came, they glided lower to caress and grip his firm bottom. She pushed full against his rising arousal and rubbed her lower half across the bulge as it thickened and grew. The feel of his solid flesh triggered tremors of desire that rushed through her body and caused her nipples to pucker and point.

Her heart pounded hard against her chest, and her core ached and pulsed with the need to feel him, hard, thick, and buried deep inside her. Desire flooded her body in a thundering tide that washed away lingering thoughts of hesitation or denial, dragging her dangerously close to the edge. Her temperature rose, and she allowed herself to get lost in the heat. Her need made her more aggressive. She pushed her face into his neck and lapped and teased his frantically beating pulse, adding fuel to his desire. Their breathing grew excited and hurried.

Suddenly, his arms closed around her like a vice and held her tight and immobile. She was elated by his unbreakable strength; every one of her senses was engaged. Her head was spinning and her nerves felt sensitive and raw. Her body surged into his and forced him backwards against the wall. Her breasts flattened against him, and her nipples, hard as bullets, poked and speared his chest. Braced against him for leverage, her hands went on an uninterrupted exploration. She gripped his arousal through his pants and rubbed, pulled, and stroked, making him moan as she devoured him with kisses and seared him with her passion.

She unzipped his pants and boldly reached inside to hold and fondle his engorged flesh, then gingerly tugged to set it free. It felt velvety smooth, hard, and hot to the touch, and it jumped and throbbed in her palm, weeping his silky liquid surrender. She clutched his shaft and lightly stroked it up and down before she delved deeper inside and gently cupped his balls. His head dropped forward, and he released his hold and leaned back against the wall, resting his hands on the railing and letting it support his weight.

"Candace." He emitted a low groan. A thin film of perspiration was visible across his forehead. "I can't think with my dick in your hands."

"Thinking is a highly overrated activity," she absently remarked as her fingers lightly grazed the head of his cock and softly squeezed his balls. "Have you ever had elevator sex, Brice?" she whispered in his ear, her warm tongue caressing his lobe and her soft hand stroking and pulling upon his still-stiffening shaft. "It can be a fascinating experience."

"I—can't say that I've had the pleasure," he choked out in a voice low and hoarse.

"You poor, poor deprived man," she breathed into the hollow of his neck. She impatiently loosened the buttons of his shirt and snatched it open to reach the hard surface and his smooth skin. She licked her way down his torso and teased his flat nipples with her tongue and teeth, continuing downward over the ridge of muscles that led the way to his navel. She paused at the top of his belted waist and looked up at him, her eyes ablaze with incredible hunger.

"Candy's going to show you what you've been missing."

She pulled his shirttail out of his pants and pressed her breasts against his warm, naked flesh. The nest of soft, fine chest hairs and bared skin brushed against the exposed skin above her satin camisole and sent a tingling sensation racing down her body, eliciting a small breathy moan. She repeated her trip down his torso and continued her sensual assault until she had his pants unbelted and hanging loose at his hips. She stared at his enlarged member and smiled before lowering her head for that long-awaited taste. His knees weakened at the gentle swipe of her tongue. She grinned in silent triumph, drew his tip into her mouth, and suckled.

His fingers automatically threaded through her hair and pulled her head down onto his shaft, and she eagerly followed his silent command. She wrapped her hand around his enlarged cock and drew it in and out of her mouth, evoking from him a ragged breath and throaty groan. She took him deeper, sucked him harder, and licked him like ice cream on a stick. His legs stiffened as he pulled her head urgently up and down onto his shaft—his head thrown back and groaning his pleasure. Then abruptly, without warning, Brice pulled her to her feet and wrapped his arms around her, breathing heavily and gripping her tight. She felt the pounding of his heart as it thudded hard against his chest and hers.

Suddenly, he whirled her around and pushed her hard against the back wall and pressed his throbbing cock at the juncture between her thighs. He buried his head in her neck, trembling and taking in large, gulping breaths, fighting a losing battle for control over his desire. She knew he'd lost that fight when he snatched her skirt up, pulled her underwear down, and thrust his fingers into her wet opening. *Yes!* She nearly collapsed from the contact as his fingers plunged inside her and his thumb rubbed circles across her aching clit. *Finally, the Ice King is melting.*

He'd gone beyond melting; he'd changed from a polar icecap to a raging volcano in the blink of an eye. He hurriedly stripped her underwear off and wedged himself between her legs again. With unbelievable strength, he lifted her up and pulled her down upon his erection, impaling her onto his shaft. He drove deep with the first thrust, so deep the sensation nearly took her over the top right then and there.

He spread her legs wider and pushed further inside and pumped his hips repeatedly with quick, mindless thrusts. She wrapped her legs around him and squeezed his body with everything she had, pulling him in up to the hilt and riding him hard. Her head and shoulders were pressed against the wall, which she allowed to support her weight. Brice slammed into her over and over, hard and fast, pushing uncontrollably into her slick, hot heat. She gave as well as she got, meeting his assault and grinding him to the base of his shaft. She held on to her dwindling sense of control for as long as she could, but as her approaching orgasm went beyond her control, she let herself go. And she pulled him over the edge with her, free-falling into the depths until they hit the current that took them faster and further than she'd ever been. They rode the wave to a mind-blowing climax that left Candace weak and gasping for air and their clothes damp with perspiration and hanging in disarray.

When his breathing was under control, Brice loosened his grip on her thighs and eased away from the wall to allow Candace to untangle her legs and stand upright. The two of them swayed precariously on weakened legs, then slid to the elevator floor. They were the perfect picture of what happens when lust is allowed to take control—him with his pants down around his knees, she with her skirt up around her waist.

"Are you okay?" he asked between breaths, as he looked down into her upturned face.

"Yes," she huffed back at him. "Barely."

"You were right. That was a hell of an experience. I'll never look at an elevator the same way again." There was a broad grin stretched across his face.

"I have a confession to make." She sat up and bit her bottom lip, suddenly uncharacteristically shy, her eyes darting off to the side. "Um, I've never actually had sex in an elevator before—only fantasies. This was my first time."

Brice stared at her for a moment in wide-eyed wonder, and then exploded into astonished laughter. "You could have fooled me. Damn, woman, you sure are full of surprises. I can't wait to find out what else is going on in that creative little mind of yours."

"Believe me, you don't want to know."

"Oh yeah?" he said, and gently turned her head toward him to look into her eyes. He smiled down at her as he brushed stray tendrils of wet hair back from her sweat-dampened cheeks. She was captivated by the warmth she now saw in his eyes. "I want to know. I want to know everything about you, but for now, we should probably get into the apartment." He frowned as he looked down at their now sweaty and badly wrinkled clothing. "I have a feeling our dinner plans may have been put on hold." He struggled to his feet and reached to help her up as well. Chuckling to himself, he pulled up his pants and buckled his belt, but didn't bother to close his shirt.

The elevator had stopped directly in front of the large double door entry to the suite. Brice fumbled in his pockets for the key, then opened the doors to reveal one of the largest expanses of open living space Candace had ever seen.

"Wow," she uttered in a low voice as her jaw dropped in wonder. *This is something out of a magazine for the rich and famous.* She stood still and took in the size and amazing view from the entry all the way to the terrace beyond. The living room, if it could be called that, looked large enough to hold at least twenty to thirty people comfortably. The dining section could be seen to the right, along with another smaller sitting area with a full bar and barstools. The entire view was alive with vibrant colors of multiple shades of red, gold, black, and brown and various textures of silk, wool, and weave. The architectural design consisted of marble floors, granite counters, beautiful columns and arches, molding, chandeliers, recessed lighting, and enormous, artfully decorated lamps. The walls were covered with several beautiful artistic pieces, and the floors were covered with equally artistic handcrafted rugs. The place looked like a freaking palace.

"Yeah, it's really something, isn't it?" His voice held a touch of pride. "Although he's retired, my dad still likes to entertain visitors and host small parties. You should see it when it's filled with people."

Candace looked around in starstruck wonder, until her eyes fell upon their disheveled reflections in a mirror that took up the entire wall on the left side of the foyer. "I think our plans for dinner are ruined." She stared in horror at the sight. "We can't possibly go out in public looking like this."

"I'm inclined to agree." Brice laughed softly at the expression on her face. "I have an idea. Let's get out of these clothes, take a shower, and order dinner from the hotel restaurant. They can deliver a gourmet meal for two, and we can even stay the night if we want."

"Stay the night? In your parents' home?" Candace crossed her arms and gave him a look that clearly said he was out of his mind. "I don't think so."

"I told you, they're traveling. Besides, I stay here off and on all the time. I still have my own room. Come on. I'll show you, and we can clean up and change into something comfortable. I'll call down for dinner." He paused and looked at their clothes again. "And the laundry service."

Brice grabbed her by the hand and dragged her down a long hallway that led to an obscenely huge bedroom that included sitting room space, a large master bath, huge walk-in closet, and sliding glass doors that led to a private terrace. Here, too, was the influence of elegance and art. Candace was again struck by the implications of wealth and privilege, and slowly started feeling like a small fish in a big pond. She was definitely swimming in waters way over her head.

"I don't have anything to change into," she said hesitantly, feeling overwhelmed.

"Sure you do. The bag you packed at your place is still in the car. I'll have the valet service send it up."

"Do you always think of everything, Brice?"

"I try to, but mostly it's habit. I told you, I'm methodical. Now, go ahead and get in the shower. I'll be right behind you as soon as I take care of those calls."

"Oh? Does that mean you plan to join me?"

"You're damned right it does." He gave her a look more meaningful and dangerous than she'd ever seen before. He pulled her into his arms and pressed a hard, demanding mouth against hers, urging her to open for him. She felt his shaft rise and stiffen again as he held her tightly. The urgency of his kiss rekindled her desire and turned her bones to mush—and pushed all those earlier uncertainties right out of her head. He pulled her skirt up and rubbed caressing strokes across her bare bottom, cupping and squeezing her cheeks, and delivered a quick stinging slap that tightened her channel and made it throb with anticipation.

"Now, go. Get in the shower," he repeated gruffly, as he broke the kiss and rubbed her bottom to take the sting away. "And don't go too far without me." He gave her a wink as he let her go and then left the room.

Chapter 17

Minutes later, Brice walked into the bathroom to find Candace standing in the spacious shower stall, her head bowed beneath the spray and her hands pressed against the wall. The sight of her nude body elicited a smile and a small sigh of satisfaction. His head filled with a hundred thoughts, and his chest filled with nearly as many unexplained emotions. They'd only just met, and yet she had him doing things he'd never anticipated. She excited and stirred his imagination. That unexpected elevator adventure was probably only a fraction of what she was capable of, and he was anxious to discover whatever else she had to offer.

He'd raided his mother's shower and brought with him lightly scented soap, shampoo, and creams to replace his masculine products. He undressed quickly, scooped up their clothes and bundled them together, and threw them outside in the hallway and locked the door. Joining her in the stall, he gave her a brief kiss on her shoulder before pouring shower gel into his hands and lathering her all over. He took his time, enjoying the slippery feeling of silky skin beneath his fingertips and savoring every stroke. He began with her shoulders, moving his hands in a circular massaging pattern, and slowly glided them down her back and over her hips. Then he turned her around to apply soap to her breasts, thighs, and between her legs, thoroughly enjoying his task. He liked the contrast of his white skin against her sun-bronzed complexion. Her full breasts and dark copper nipples enticed him.

"This is nice. You have great hands." She sighed and relaxed into the sensation he created with talented fingers and gentle pressure.

"Yeah, I know. It gets better."

"Better than this? I don't know if I can stand better." She laughed softly.

"I'm willing to bet you can stand more than you think," he responded in a low, husky voice.

He lathered and washed every exposed inch of her body while delivering soft, sensual, lingering kisses on her lips, ears, and throat. When she was covered entirely in whipped peaks of scented soapy lather, he turned his attention to himself. Candace took her turn assisting, lathering, laughing, and enjoying the mutual exploration of their bodies. She leaned against his chest and circled her arms around his neck, both covered in soap, slipping and sliding against one another and sharing deep, ravenous kisses underneath the steady shower spray.

Eventually, he reached for the handheld nozzle and began to rinse away the soapy residue. He turned her around and pulled her back against him and changed the setting on the showerhead from spray to pulsating, then moved the warm water down her body, over her breasts and stomach, and down to her smooth, clean shaven mound. She gasped. He felt her shiver from the sudden shock of warmth and pressure as it pulsed directly over her clit. Her nipples hardened and pointed. His erection was at full attention and pressed firmly against her backside, nestled comfortably in that now familiar resting place. He liked the way his shaft automatically fit the curve of her bottom.

The showerhead pounded a continuous throbbing force against that most sensitive area while he delivered hot wet kisses to her neck and shoulder. He reached between her legs and spread her nether lips with one hand and turned the spray at an angle for a direct, continual assault on her pleasure button. She squirmed and pushed back against him. The intensity of the pulsating water made her shudder as the pinpoint precision of the spray struck her with forceful repetition. Her nipple buds grew harder, and the muscles in her thighs and legs were stiff. She stretched and writhed in struggle against the feeling, and he held on to her throughout the fight.

"It's okay, Candy. I've got you. Let go," he whispered in her ear. The sound of her moans rose with her conflict. His embrace tightened as he felt her lose control and give into an orgasm that rushed through her with an overwhelming, shattering intensity. Experiencing her climax with her was nearly as potent and debilitating for him. Brice held her until they both recovered, pressing light kisses on her neck and cheek and whispering sweet nonsense in her ear until she was able to move.

They toweled off with huge spa towels and then went into the bedroom. Brice pulled a pair of black silk pajamas out of the drawer and gave her the top while he put on the bottom with one of his undershirts. They stood for a moment, embracing and kissing, until he took her hand and led her back toward the entry to the residence. There, they found her personal bag had been placed inside the doorway, their clothes were gone, and an entire meal had been set up on the kitchen counter and placed inside electric warmers. The dining table had been set for two with silverware, plates and glasses, and a bottle of wine chilling inside an ice bucket.

"Where did all this come from?" She looked around in awe.

"Someone from the hotel staff set it up."

"You mean there was someone here while we were in the shower?"

"Yes."

"There was someone here, besides us?"

He saw the brief look of fear in her eyes and suddenly realized what must be going through her head. She was still spooked by the recent break-in.

"Yes. It's okay, Candace, that's what they do. They are trusted employees who take care of the residents. It's part of the service here, if requested." He wrapped his arms around her and pulled her in close to calm her. "Remember I told you I was going to make some calls? I asked them to bring us dinner."

• • •

"Mm, this is so good." She licked her lips and reached for another serving. "Aren't you going to have any more?"

"No." He pushed his chair back and reached for his glass of wine. "I'm saving room for dessert."

"There's dessert? I didn't see any dessert." She creased her brows and surveyed the banquet of food and drink spread out on the table. When she turned toward him with a questioning look on her face, he eyed her pointedly with one eyebrow raised.

"Ooh." A wicked smile spread across her face and sparkled in her eyes. "Well, in that case ... " Candace hurriedly pushed all the dishes to one side, climbed onto the table, and crawled over and sat at the end, directly in front of Brice. She took his wine glass out of his hand, took a sip, and put it aside, then wrapped her arms around his neck. "Dessert is served."

Brice grinned from ear to ear as he pulled her down onto his lap. He leaned in to kiss her, and let his hands roam and explore her body until they settled around her breasts, cupping their weight and brushing her nipples with his thumbs and teasing them with his tongue. Finally he stood, and she wrapped her legs around his waist. His erection stood high and pressed intimately against her panty-covered divide. He nuzzled her neck.

"I think I'll have my dessert 'to go.'"

"Shouldn't we clear the table?" She quivered; the thrill from such brazen contact warmed her blood and made her tingle deep down inside.

"Don't worry about it. The service center will send someone up tomorrow to take care of it when they bring breakfast. Grab that bottle and those glasses. We're going to need something to quench our thirst later." He carried her off to his room, his hands gripping her bottom with her legs clamped around his waist, her face buried in his neck, laughing and giggling all the way.

• • •

"Oh, oh, oh, ouch!"

"What?"

"I think I have a cramp."

"Where?"

"Right ... there." She pointed to the calf of her left leg.

"Don't be such a baby."

"But it hurts."

"That's what you get for acting like a gymnast. I told you that last move was probably too risqué." Brice laughed as he massaged her leg with firm, intense pressure.

"A simple 'I told you so' would be sufficient. You don't need to torture me to get the point across."

"You're going to thank me when this is over."

"Yeah, that's what they all say." She grumbled and gritted her teeth against the pain. "You're just trying to justify your sadism."

He made her turn over on her back. Placing her foot on his shoulder, he massaged her entire leg from her thigh down to her toes.

She'd never admit it, but he was right. She could already feel the muscles in her whole body relaxing from the all-over warm oil massage he was giving her. She'd never felt so pampered in her life. She'd spent the last forty-eight hours living one of those so-called fairy tales. She'd been rescued by a handsome prince and taken to his castle and waited on hand and foot. Literally. If she wasn't careful, she just might start believing in all that fairy tale hype.

While she wasn't quite ready to fall for the fairy princess in wonderland propaganda yet, she would admit to one thing: the last forty-eight hours with Brice had been eye-opening. He'd shown her what it was like to be with a sweet, caring, and considerate man. A taste of what she'd been missing in life had her seriously questioning the sound practice of her fool-proof plan. After a night of blissful intercourse, by turns making love and laughing, talking about nothing and everything, she'd be hard pressed to go back to her bottom-of-the-barrel bad habits.

"You know what I just realized?" she asked, basking in the sensation of him massaging the arch of her foot and pulling on her toes.

"What's that?"

"That technically we're still on our second date. I've never had a date that lasted an entire weekend. And the funny thing is though it's only been a few short weeks, it feels like we've actually known each other since, oh, I don't know—forever?"

"Yeah, I know what you mean. We click. I think that's what they call chemistry."

She sighed and propped herself up on her elbows to watch as he massaged her foot. "I suppose chemistry's as good an explanation as any, but it's a shame you're such a nice guy."

His hands went still and his eyebrows rose as he pinned her with a level stare. "What's wrong with being a nice guy?"

"There's nothing 'wrong' with it. I simply make it a point to avoid them like the plague."

"Why?"

"Because I'm not interested in a relationship, and nice guys usually want something more stable than a couple of nights rolling around between the sheets. I've already been there, done that. It didn't work out, and I moved on. I have no intention of making the same mistake again." She wasn't being entirely honest, but she didn't see any point in bringing up the past. The truth was she didn't trust nice. But she didn't owe him the truth.

Brice resumed his massage. "If you're trying to tell me something, Candace, I'm all ears."

She returned his steady gaze and decided to broach the idea she'd been turning over in her head.

"Look, Brice, we've only known each other for a little while. And at this point, there's not much between us except a little conversation and a lot of physical attraction. But before this goes any further I have to ask. You're not interested in anything long-term, are you? I mean, what we're doing now is fine. Right? You've as much as admitted you're a confirmed bachelor, not ready to settle down. And I'm not looking to change your status—or mine." Staring into those icy-cool and incredibly blue eyes was starting to make her feel just a tad nervous. She would start squirming any minute.

"Go on."

"I have a proposal to make that could fit into both our plans." Her eyes shifted to focus on her toes while she spoke. "Since it's obvious we get along and we like each other in and out of the bedroom, why don't we make this a friends-with-benefits relationship? You know, no strings attached. We spend time together whenever we want, but still have the freedom and flexibility to date others as well. If it gets to a point where one of us develops feelings more than friendship, we cut it off before it gets complicated, like an exit clause or something."

She continued, somewhat unsteadily: "You said you're a man who doesn't like drama. I don't think things could get any more drama-free than that. This could be the perfect arrangement, a win-win situation. What do you think?" She lifted her eyes to gauge his reaction. He didn't look at her directly as he continued his massage, but it appeared he was at least considering her proposal.

"I think you might be onto something," he finally responded as he carefully released her leg and moved to lie down beside her. He took her hand into his and kissed her knuckles and gave her a devilish smile. "I have to admit I'm a little shocked. It's not every day a guy meets a girl who isn't interested in a one-on-one relationship. Are you telling me you have *zero* interest in making our connection exclusive?"

"Yep, that's exactly what I'm saying."

"Sounds like you've got it all worked out. But have you ever heard the saying 'The best laid plans of mice and men often go astray'?"

"Yes, I've heard it, but I never really understood the meaning."

"It means that no matter how well you might plan something, there's always a chance for the unexpected to happen. In other words, just because you *think* things will go as planned, odds are they can still go wrong."

"I'm sure you're right, under normal circumstances." She flipped him over and straddled his body, pressing her breasts flat against his chest and wrapping her arms around his neck. "But if we both focus on the *friendship* and the *benefits* of this arrangement" she said, punctuating the two words with a slow grind of her lower body, "how could anything possibly go wrong?"

"Well, since you put it that way," he responded in a husky voice as he guided his hardened length into her soft, moist channel. "I'm more than willing to take a chance on beating the odds."

Chapter 18

Brice stood as still as a statue in the middle of his kitchen, a bottle of beer in one hand and the other stuffed deep in his jeans pocket. He stared into nothingness as he relived the past seventy-two hours. Leaving her on her doorstep had been the hardest thing he'd ever had to do. He'd tried every angle he could think of short of kidnapping, but he couldn't convince her to stay with him any longer. She'd said thank you very much, but three days were enough. She had to go back and face her house, and she had a job and other responsibilities. She wouldn't even let him come inside to help her clear away the mess and damage left behind, insisting that she do it on her own.

Even though he'd dropped her off only a few hours ago, it bothered him to know she was there all alone. Her eyes still held remnants of fear and uncertainty, and even with new locks and a new alarm system, he could tell she didn't feel safe in her own home. Although he'd much rather have her stay with him a while longer, he was proud of her determination and refusal to let fear rule her life. But he wanted to protect her. He wanted to keep her safe.

He didn't dare push her, especially not now after that ridiculous arrangement she'd suggested. Her proposal had caught him completely off-guard, contradicting everything he thought he knew about women. Had it come from anyone but Candace, he would have jumped all over the opportunity with no problem and no questions asked. It was the kind of agreement every commitment-phobic man dreamed of.

Generally his relationships fell into one of two categories. He either went the whole nine yards from the chase and romance angle—until the feeling wore off, prompting him to spout the standard nonsense about how it wasn't working for him, he needed space, blah, blah, blah. Or, there was the typical one-night stand, when almost anyone with a pulse would do because he needed to get laid. He'd never wanted more than that. It was his MO to turn tail and run at the first rumblings of "when are we going take this to the next level?" Now with the shoe on the other foot, he wasn't so sure he liked how it fit.

What was his hesitation? Was his ego bruised over the thought that a woman was ready to dump *him* at the first signs of emotional dependency? Or was it because, finally, for the first time in his life, he might be interested in more than a casual fling or a one-night stand?

The beeping of his phone interrupted his attempt at self-psychoanalysis. He answered right away when he saw the caller was Rick Thorne.

"Hello, Rick."

"Hi, Brice. I've acquired the information you requested." As usual Rick got right to the point in his strictly business manner.

"Let's hear it."

"Andrew Nash lives in New York City, in the upscale Manhattan neighborhood of Chelsea. He is regional director for a medical supply manufacture-and-distribution chain, run by a multimillion-dollar corporation. He is in charge of the southeast region of the U.S., and travels at least once a quarter to North Carolina, South Carolina, Georgia, and Alabama to personally oversee plant services and operations. His annual salary is approximately $375,000 a year, not including bonuses. He spends his money on expensive hobbies such as casino gambling, sports betting, fast women, and faster cars. His overindulgences have brought him close to the brink of financial disaster on several occasions; however, so far he's managed to keep his head above water.

"In recent weeks, he adjusted his travel schedule to visit Atlanta on average at least twice a month, citing a sick relative living in the area as the reason. He's been in Atlanta twice in the last three weeks; his most recent visit was this week. He stayed at the Ritz-Carlton downtown, which appears to be his preferred place of residence when in town. He departed on Sunday morning at eight a.m. on a return flight to New York City."

"What about criminal history? Does he have a record? Has he ever been arrested?"

"I had to dig deep. Someone very adept at hiding information buried it under layers and layers of administrative data, but he's had a string of harassment complaints filed against him in every state in his region of operation. But he apparently must have connections within the system because all of the incidents were dismissed, documented as minor infractions, or swept under the carpet to disappear altogether."

"He's even more of an asshole than I thought," Brice muttered. "And an asshole with connections can be a dangerous combination."

"There's more."

"I'm listening."

"He's former military. He was a captain in the Marine Corps and served one full four-year enlistment and two years of a second term, which ended when he was discharged for conduct unbecoming an officer. His military occupational specialty was as an intelligence officer, which means he's probably trained in surveillance, counter surveillance, and other information-gathering techniques. For the most part, he was a desk jockey and wouldn't have seen any real action. I don't have all the details of his discharge, but I did learn he was accused of sexual harassment and assault. The assault charges didn't stick.

"His psych evaluation prior to dismissal confirms my initial personality assessment. The doctor diagnosed Nash as having narcissistic personality disorder, also referred to as NPD, as well as possible symptoms of paranoia or schizophrenia."

"What does that mean, Rick? Is he dangerous?"

"NPD is a disorder with varying degrees of severity. Some have an underlying need for dominance and derive immense pleasure from others' suffering. They view themselves as special, have self-aggrandizing thoughts, and don't believe that rules apply to them. They have no empathy and don't possess a sense of guilt. Basically, they don't have a conscience.

"I believe your friend Nash fits this profile. He is accustomed to using manipulation and control to get what he wants, and once he's fixated on someone, he will refuse to relinquish his hold. Relationships, if they can be characterized as such, end on his terms, and he will undoubtedly ignore any attempts to cut him loose. I also believe Nash is a borderline psychopath with a consuming hatred for women. He sees them as property to be controlled. Your friend was lucky she dumped him when she did; however, his history indicates he will refuse to accept that the relationship is over.

"This disorder didn't just happen overnight, Brice. I'm certain that this behavior manifested itself years prior to his diagnosis, which means he's had a lifetime to refine his ability to mask his true self. To answer your question—absolutely, yes. The man is potentially very dangerous."

"Why would a man with a military-intelligence background end up in the field of medicine? That doesn't make sense to me."

"I agree, but an unbecoming conduct discharge carries a lot of weight in the civilian world. Nash comes from a family of physicians and pharmacists, so working in the medical field would have been his fallback plan."

Brice had grown increasingly tense as he heard each revelation. He could only imagine the hell he'd put those other women through, but he'd be damned if he'd let that scum do the same thing to Candace.

"I want to know his whereabouts this past Friday night, and I want to know where he is now," Brice said tightly.

"I obtained a record of incoming and outgoing calls made from his cell phone for the last thirty days. If you'll provide me with your friend's address, I can check for any calls bouncing off of cell towers within a ten-mile radius of her home, and what time they were made. As for his current whereabouts, I can put a team on him right away and advise you if he makes a return trip to Atlanta."

"Do it."

Brice gave Rick the information he needed and hung up the phone. He needed a stronger drink. The report had left a bad taste in his mouth. Nash was the lowest kind of scum that walked the earth. He'd gotten away with his terror tactics for too long—and obviously believed he was untouchable. But those women hadn't had Brice to look after them. He would keep a closer eye on Candace whether she wanted him to or not.

Once he resolved to take on the role of her personal protector, his thoughts turned to more serious concerns. He knew Candace felt nothing for him other than maybe a growing friendship. Truthfully, it was way too soon to have expectations. But *his* world had started unraveling long before she'd put her proposition on the table.

He was willing to go along with it—for now. He'd do whatever it took to keep her in his bed while he worked his way into her heart. Meanwhile, he'd make sure she had no reason to be with another man. It gave him a headache to even consider the possibility. Maybe in that one aspect alone he grudgingly understood Nash's insane obsession—he didn't want to share her with anyone else.

Chapter 19

Candace sat looking out of her living room window, brooding over a hot cup of tea. It had been weeks since the break-in, and things were starting to feel almost normal again. But the police still had nothing—whoever trashed her place had left no evidence behind. The more she thought about it, the more she wondered if there might be something to Brice's suspicions. Was Nash responsible for the damage to her home? Brice was right about the destruction: it had a vicious, personal element to it. Had Nash been so pissed off at her that he would respond in such a way? It was hard to comprehend that much anger and violence directed solely toward her—or that he'd go so far out of some distorted sense of revenge.

But, with no arrests or suspects, she was forced to accept there'd be no justice. She'd put on a brave face and picked up the broken pieces, cleaned up the mess, and tried to pull her life back together. But despite her best efforts to go back to how things were before, she couldn't get beyond the stab of fear she felt each time she unlocked her door. She jumped at imaginary noises, left lights on in every room, and propped a chair against her bedroom door before going to bed, just in case.

Brice called nearly every day. Despite the warning signs of moving too fast and getting too close, she looked forward to every call and hearing the sound of his voice.

So far, he was doing a pretty good job of living up to his role as her knight in shining armor, with the added bonus of good sex to keep her mind off her fear. *Wait, did I say "good" sex? I meant "rolling in the sheets sweating out my hair and waking the neighbors with screaming O's" sex.* Yeah, the kind that made your toes curl and your legs cramp up. Even with her own aggressive nature and voracious appetite, she was finding it hard to keep up. Who knew that unexpected tryst in the elevator would melt the Ice King and release such an insatiable monster? The man might have artic-cold eyes that seemed to look right through you, but there was molten lava running through his veins. At times, she felt exposed and stripped bare beneath his perceptive gaze. And the feeling scared her shitless.

His concern and thoughtfulness melted her insides and gave her that special, cared-for feeling. But "special" and "cared-for" were feelings she didn't want to get used to. Brice needed to be kept at arm's length, or further. Her brilliant friends-with-benefits agreement might not have been such a sure bet. There was no guarantee she wouldn't do something foolish—like get blindsided by emotional stupidity—and mistake just having a good time for something more. It wouldn't be the first time. When it came to matters of the heart, she knew she had a poor track record for making sensible choices. She'd made a fool of herself, twice. Perhaps the first time could be excused because of youth and the lack of experience. But the second time around, she should have known better. She should have learned her lesson—that toying with a woman's emotions was just part of the game men liked to play.

Maybe after all these years, her resistance to relationships had more to do with pride than pain. She wasn't really sure anymore. The one thing she knew for certain was that she wasn't going to play the fool ever again. Humiliation was a hard pill to swallow. She wouldn't let seemingly sweet considerations and warm and fuzzy sensations weasel their way into her heart—again. There was a reason she held onto her pain like a favorite pair of old shoes. It was her reminder that the heart couldn't be trusted to make sound decisions.

Candace glanced at the clock and sighed heavily. It was time to push Brice and bad premonitions aside. Right now she had other concerns, and they would be knocking on her door any minute. Joyce and Sarona were on their way over for a girls' night out. They'd called and insisted on seeing her, and although she'd tried all kinds of excuses to keep them away—she didn't feel up to a night out, answering a million questions or being pitied—they wouldn't take no for an answer. When her doorbell rang at eight o'clock, they stood on her doorstep with overstuffed arms and bright smiles.

• • •

"The place looks good, Candy," Sarona said from her position on the floor, lounging in silk shorty pajamas and sitting among a mass of comforters, sheets, and pillows. The girls had moved the furniture aside and laid down makeshift pallets on the living room floor. A small table in the center of the room was covered with bottles of wine, champagne, and cocktail mix along with fruit, chocolate, and cheese. They were all set for a fun-filled night of uninhibited eating, drinking, and uncensored girl talk, and all three were lounging around in PJs with glasses in hand. "You can't even tell there's been a break-in."

"Thanks. I've tried to put it behind me and get my life back to normal. But it just doesn't feel the same anymore. It doesn't feel like home. It feels almost tainted now—violated. *I* feel violated."

"Oh baby, I'm so sorry." Sarona leaned over and hugged her hard. "What did the police say?"

"Not much. They don't have any leads. There's just nothing to go on to take the investigation any further."

"How are you holding up?"

"I'm okay. The hardest part is being here alone after dark. It's awful to feel this uncomfortable in my own home." She shrugged and let out a small sigh. "But Brice has been a big help with seeing me through it."

"Brice? Who's Brice?" Sarona sat up in surprise. "I've been out of touch for only a few weeks, and suddenly there's somebody named *Brice* in your life? What did I miss?"

"Sorry, dear. We haven't had time to catch you up," Joyce responded. "You've been drowning in David for the last month, so we thought we'd wait until you came up for air."

"Joke all you want, Ms. Jeffers, but it's your fault I'm suddenly rooted in this sordid life of endless sex and scandal—you with your 'life is about chances' speech, for which I'm eternally grateful." Sarona giggled into her glass. "So, *tell* me. What happened while I was gone?"

"Oh, nothing much, except that our girl Candace hooked up with a really gorgeous hunk of man-flesh: tall, dark, and oh-so-handsome—kind of like your guy. And he's become her self-appointed guardian."

"Details, ladies, I need details. Starting with the how, when, and what's next?"

There was a brief moment of silence, and then all three women burst into gales of laughter.

"Slow your roll, girlfriend, let's not get ahead of ourselves. Let's just stick with the 'how and when' and the here and now, okay?" Candace and Joyce filled Sarona in on the story of her and Brice. They explained how he'd plotted their meeting, his gallant rescue the night of the break-in, followed by his chivalrous invitation and her weekend stay at his place.

"Wait. Did you say Brice Coleman?"

"Yeah? Why?" Candace asked with one eyebrow raised.

"OMG! That's David's partner. You've been going out with David's partner."

"What are you talking about?"

"David's security consulting service! He and his friend Brice are old college buds who decided to go into business together.

Holy crap! Talk about a small world." Sarona practically fell over from laughing so hard.

Candace was floored. This was not good news. As if she didn't already have enough problems with Sarona hounding her at every turn. With David's connection to Brice, now there'd be no end to her meddling attempts to push her into a relationship.

"This is just so romantic, and it has all the perfect ingredients to turn into something wonderful," Sarona gushed.

"Wait. Hold on now. I can see how you might think that, but it's not like that," Candace hurriedly interrupted. "Brice and I were sort of pushed into this thing because of what happened, but we have a strictly friends-with-benefits arrangement. It's not exclusive, and we prefer it that way. Neither of us is interested in a commitment. So, you can stop right now with any plans forming in that head of yours to stir up trouble."

"Oh, Candy, how can you say that? I can't believe you don't want something that gives you that forever-after feeling. Don't you want someone in your life you can count on? Brice sounds like he's that kind of guy. He could be the perfect candidate for your Mr. Right."

Candace rolled her eyes at Sarona's unfailing and ridiculous belief in fantasies. "Don't talk to me about Mr. Right. Mr. Right is nothing more than a fairy tale, orchestrated and perpetuated by the media and commercial enterprises, packaged in a fancy container, and shoved down our throats as the gospel truth. I have a news flash for you, Sarona: I'm not interested in finding Mr. Right. Misters 'Right Now' and 'Maybe Later' will do me just fine."

Chapter 20

Rick put a surveillance team on Nash and reported his whereabouts to Brice at least once a week. Nash had made two trips to Atlanta in the last month, but he hadn't tried to contact Candace at all. Brice didn't know what his game was, but he knew enough not to trust him. With the information from Brice, Rick had linked Candace's address with data from cell towers located in the area. He'd pinpointed two outgoing calls from Nash's phone on the night of the break-in. Both calls placed him practically on her doorstep. If Brice had ever had a shred of doubt that Nash was responsible for the destruction of her property and sense of security, this latest report eliminated it completely. But no matter how sure he was of Nash's guilt, this new information only left him feeling more frustrated and helpless.

Because, unfortunately, it wasn't evidence that he'd committed a crime. It wasn't against the law to park on a public street in front of her home. Brice continued poring over the reports searching for something, anything he could use to flush Nash out, when finally something caught his attention. He recognized the name of the company Nash worked for. Here was something that might possibly work to his advantage.

Brice picked up his saxophone and began absently stroking the keys while he considered his next move. Nash took great pleasure in harassing people and making their lives miserable. *Maybe he should have a taste of what it feels like when the tables are turned.* Brice knew people—people who could ask questions, make insinuations, and stir up all manner of trouble for somebody with a questionable or unsavory background. He reached for the phone.

"Hi, Blaine. It's Brice. Got a minute?"

"Yeah, sure, man. What's up?"

"I've got a problem, and I think maybe you can help me solve it."

"Well, let's hear what you got."

"It's kind of complicated. I don't want to go into it over the phone."

"Okay then, come by the office."

"This isn't an office kind of visit. It's personal. Let me buy you lunch, and we can discuss it."

"Sounds serious."

"It is."

"How about Casio's? Tomorrow, say, around noon?"

"That'll be great. I'll see you there."

• • •

Brice arrived early and was waiting when Blaine showed up fifteen minutes later. They ordered drinks and their meal before getting down to the reason for the meeting.

"So tell me, my man, what can I do for you? You sounded pretty grim over the phone."

"I'll get right to the point," Brice said after taking a long swig from his drink. "Remember the last time we saw each other, just after you'd gotten back into town?"

"Oh yeah. How could I forget? You were having dinner with that fine sister, and I was jealous as hell," he joked. "I remember some guy tried to make a move on her while you were hanging with me. I watched you two have a faceoff, and then he left."

"That's why I called you. The situation is still ongoing. Her name is Candace, and the guy is a former lover who's turned into a big problem for her—and me."

"Wait. It's been what, nearly two months since that night. Are you telling me you're still with the same woman ... for two months?" Blaine sat back in his seat, apparently in shock.

Brice winced inwardly at his friend's surprise. "Yes, it's been about that," he responded evenly. He had no intention of discussing the details of their relationship, but he would have to give up something if he was going to ask for help. "We've been seeing each other off and on for a while. I like her company, and she likes mine. And the sex is great. The problem is that a while back her house was broken into and vandalized, and I have every reason to believe it was the guy from the restaurant."

"How did you come to that conclusion?" Blaine asked.

"The guy is an asshole. I knew it the moment I met him. She already ended the relationship, and he's been harassing her ever since."

Brice explained how his suspicions had prompted him to call his private investigator, and then he quietly filled Blaine in on the specifics of Rick's report. He conveniently left out his invitation to stay for the weekend. He wasn't about to admit to the overwhelming feelings he was developing for her—or the fast and furious emotional ride he'd been on since that fateful first meeting.

"The incriminating information Rick's gathered on this guy doesn't bode well for Candace. I don't think she's heard the last of him. According to Rick, the break-in is a warning that things could escalate. He needs to be stopped. Considering his mental state of mind and hidden criminal past, I'm concerned he might not stop at just trying to scare her."

"What did the police say?"

"Unfortunately, the lack of incriminating evidence ruled out any help from the police. I'm left to employ my own methods of protecting Candace." Brice spoke with cold, calculating calmness. "Andrew Nash needs to be taught a couple of lessons. One, that he's not the only person capable of screwing with someone's life, and two, that he won't keep getting away with it. I want him to know what it feels like to have his life turned upside down for no reason." The look in Brice's eyes hardened. "I want him to know what it feels like to be fucked with."

"Okay, so let's say you're right. What do you need me for?"

"He has a high-profile job in the medical industry with a pristine reputation to look out for, which means he can't afford rumors or accusations to come to light. The way I see it, this is right up your alley, seeing as how your law firm happens to represent the same company." Brice dropped that little bombshell and picked up his drink to take another swallow. "You'd be duty-bound to uphold company policy and inform them of indiscrete behavior within the ranks. You know, to prevent potential lawsuits, complaints, things of that nature."

Blaine's eyes narrowed with interest at Brice's revelation.

"Are you saying this nutcase works for us?"

"Yeah, well, he works for your client. And I'm guessing this is the type of information they'd want to be made aware of. Am I right?"

Blaine gave Brice a probing look. "I'll need a copy of that report. I can't make allegations without something to back them up."

"I'll have Rick send it to your office."

"I'll also need copies of the police report and any photos taken of the damage. The more information I have, the better the case I can build against him."

"I told you, there's no proof he's responsible."

"It doesn't matter. If I can plant a seed of suspicion in the minds of the board members, that's all I need to set the ball rolling. Hey, I'm a lawyer. He doesn't have to be tried in a court of law. The court of public opinion is way more effective when it comes to handing out judgment."

"Thanks, man. I'm glad you're willing to check this out. But I want you to hold off on taking any action just yet. You're my ace in the hole, and I'm not ready to show my hand."

"No problem, I can do that. But I still want that information as soon as possible to conduct my own investigation. What about Candace?"

"What about her?" Brice was suddenly defensive.

"I want to know her role in all of this. How do you know she didn't do something to set this guy off? Maybe she pushed him and didn't realize he had a short fuse. Or maybe she's using you to get an old lover off her back. Are you sure she's worth all the time and trouble you're putting into this?"

"She didn't do anything to set this fucker off. He's a mental case, plain and simple. It was just her bad luck she ended up with the wrong guy. She's not 'using me' because she doesn't even know that I had him investigated. And yes. She's worth every second of my time and trouble."

Chapter 21

It had been two weeks since they'd made love, and Brice was practically going out of his mind with wanting her. He'd never, ever before in his life *needed* sex. Sex was a pastime, a means to satisfy an urge and take the edge off, and there was no shortage of willing partners just waiting for his call. *Need* was never a part of the equation. This new inability to control his desire and fantasies was shocking—and unsettling.

He'd lain awake too many nights imagining her supple body lying beneath him, supine, submissive, and open to his touch, his invasion. He visualized her beautiful face twisted in pleasure as he surged in deep and steadily pushed her to the brink of her endurance and beyond. And when she fell over the edge, out of control and writhing in his arms, he shivered at the sound of her voice as it rang out sweetly and she sang her orgasm in his ears.

Brice brushed a hand over his face and groaned out loud while his cock twitched and throbbed painfully to life. The memory of her moist channel gripping him hard and squeezing tight, pulsating around his thickened member as she milked him dry, nearly drove him insane.

Her essence was a living thing that vibrated in the air around him. Her natural scent of honey and spice lingered in his nose and filled his mouth with the sweetness of her taste. The thought of her made him burn and ache for her tang and touch. She'd slipped under his skin and inside his heart without warning. Candace was like a drug. He'd gotten hooked with his first adventurous taste, and like an addict he was stuck on the edge between what was imagined or real, desperate for his next fix.

He reached for the phone to call her, unable to resist the pull that drew him in against his will. He had to hear her voice. As he punched in the number, his defiant claim to David that he "wasn't going down without a fight" rang loudly in his ears. Where was that grit and determination now? For all his bluff and bluster, he hadn't put forth much effort to salvage his pride or his freedom.

"I don't believe you've been keeping up your end of our friends-with-benefits agreement," he said when she answered the phone.

"What do you mean?"

"I want to see you. I'm tired of waiting and hearing that you're too busy to make time for me. With all these excuses, if I didn't know better I'd think you were avoiding me. I'm a patient man, Candace, and I don't normally think with my dick, but lately all I can think about is having you in my bed, lying under me with your hands tangled in my hair and your legs wrapped around my waist. I want to be in your arms and buried deep inside you. Right now."

His voice, deliberately pitched low and husky, exuded an infinite hunger intended to make her toes curl and her vaginal walls twitch and contract. He knew what it did to her. He dropped his voice lower and practically growled into the phone. He wasn't beyond playing dirty or pulling out all the stops. Why should he be the only one suffering?

"I think I've been a damn good friend over the past few weeks, but I haven't received any of those benefits we discussed. You've been holding out on me, babe. This was your idea, and I intend to reap my fair share of those promised rewards."

"I'm sorry. How incredibly inconsiderate of me," she responded playfully. The sound of her teasing laughter rang in his ear. The familiar feeling of heat gathered in his gut and went straight to his groin, stabbing him with a thousand painful bursts of red-hot pleasure. "I didn't realize I was in breach of our agreement."

"How can you live without me? You do it so well, and it bothers me," he replied gruffly, his tight control unraveling further at the melodic sound of her voice. "Woman, don't make me beg. I expect to see you tonight, and the only thing I need to hear from you is 'My place or yours?'"

"Um, I think playtime at your place will be perfect. I love romping around in that playground you call a king-sized bed. And," she breathed wickedly into the phone, "I can't wait to see the master in his master bedroom."

His blood pressure spiked and his temperature rose as the sleeping dominant in him raised its head and stirred. "Be careful what you ask for. I may feel obliged to see that you get it."

"Um, sounds kinky. I *like* kinky."

"Good. That's what I'm counting on. I'll see you around eight o'clock. And Candace—don't be late."

He hung up the phone grinning and bursting with excitement. It was time to move this relationship forward, but he would have to tread carefully. Instinct warned him that getting her to even consider the possibility was as dangerous as walking through a minefield, and it could lead to an explosion of monumental proportions.

• • •

Brice constantly surprised her with his uncensored honesty. He held nothing back. He spoke his mind and got straight to the point. His frank admission of desire, and the sound of his voice—hard, edged with need, and full of demand—made her hot. Blatant talk of his need for her made her nipples stiff and bead tightly, and, God help her, she needed to change her underwear. She wanted him just as much, but she wasn't nearly as open and honest about it as he was.

He was right. She *had* been avoiding him. She wasn't immune to his sweet touch and his thoughtful ways. She'd been doomed from the start, when he'd first wrapped himself around her and held her all night long, just to comfort her. She'd felt it then for the first time, that elusive feeling women dream of, the feeling of being safe, protected, and cared for. It had been the same ever since. Every time they'd made love and stayed together, she'd wake in the morning enclosed in his arms, tangled in his legs, and surrounded by his scent. It was addictive, that feeling of being safe and wanted. It was something a girl could get used to.

Her mind and body craved him, and she constantly fought unpredictable and overpowering urges to run to him as often as she truly wanted to. There was no denying it; she was totally hooked on the man and how he made her feel, the way he made love to her. The way he touched, teased, and made her body come alive was wonderful—and frightening. In a desperate attempt to hold onto her heart, she tried to keep her distance. But it wasn't working. It didn't matter that she told him lies and tried to stay away. She couldn't lie to herself. His cool blue eyes and warm smile had drawn her in, and she ached to be wrapped inside his strong arms.

This no-strings, no-commitment arrangement was getting harder and harder to live with, but changing the rules was not an option. She might lose her head and control of her body, but losing her heart was non-negotiable.

• • •

She rang the doorbell at precisely eight o'clock, her heart hammering with excitement. Brice opened the door and immediately pulled her inside. He wrapped his arms around her and kissed her hard and deep, pouring his need into her and filling her up. He surrounded her, consuming her with his passion. He kissed her long and with unrestrained fervor, until she realized that there was no gentle teasing, no quiet laughter, no calming reassurance. This man in her arms was someone she didn't recognize. And it excited her.

When he finally released her, he retreated and let his hands drop to his sides, breathing heavily as if struggling for control. The intensity of his kiss and the strength of his embrace left her swaying and nearly breathless. She kept her eyes closed, feeling electrically charged, slightly disoriented, and burning from the inside out. When she was able to force her eyes open, she was surprised by what she saw. He was dressed entirely in black: black jeans, a black t-shirt stretched taunt across his muscular chest, black biker boots, and black leather bands wrapped around his wrists. He looked rugged, sexy, seductive, and scary. His dark presence excited her. This new look was a far cry from his usual custom-tailored suits and silk ties. He looked more forceful, more powerful, more dominating, more masculine—more *everything*. She nervously licked her lower lip.

"Do you trust me, Candace?" He placed both hands on her arms and brushed over them in a long, sensual sweep from her shoulders down to her fingertips, and threaded their fingers together. Again she licked her lower lip, uncertain of the answer. Did she trust him? She was afraid of the intense heat and the dangerous look that smoldered in his eyes, and yet, inexplicably drawn to the exciting promise of both. Her fear of losing control was far outweighed by her excitement. Something deep inside warned her she was on the verge of a discovery that could change her life forever, but she couldn't bring herself to resist. She swallowed hard, and nodded her head.

"There's something wild in you, Candace, something that's been contained and misunderstood for too long. I want to help you let it out. Will you trust me with that?" Again she nodded. "I have something for you."

He took her hand and pulled her further into the house. The room was dimly lit with recessed lighting from above, further enhanced with the glow of several candles scattered about. He kissed her again, this one lingering, tender, and more sedate than the previous one. He handed her a large box with a black top, pink-and-black stripes along the sides, and a black bow tying the two together. The name of the store, Straight Up with a Twist, was embossed in raised gold script across the top. "I went shopping and picked up a few things. I want you to put these on."

Her eyes widened with surprise and she gave him a questioning look, but his blank expression gave nothing away. She removed the top and cautiously peeked inside. Carefully peeling back delicate pink tissue paper, she revealed a black latex harness bra with tiny pink bows stitched below each shoulder strap, and two black latex pasties to cover the nipples once the breasts hung exposed and free. Included was a matching pair of extremely short shorts with a zipper that ran from the rear, through the crotch, and ended in front just below the waist. And finally, there was a pair of black round-toed six-inch platform heels with red-bottomed soles.

Candace looked at the contents of the box in stunned silence and a growing excitement. She pulled out the harness bra and ran her hands over the shiny black material. She felt something deep inside unfurl and purr with recognition and expectation. "Where should I change?" she asked in a low voice as she pulled each piece from the box and carefully set them aside.

"Right here. I want to watch."

Without hesitation she began to strip, taking her time to savor the sensation of icy blue eyes fixated on her every move. He stood with his legs apart, his hands clasped together, and his head slightly bowed, watching as she took her time and slowly removed each piece of clothing. He shamelessly wrapped his hand around the thickness of his stiffening cock, gripping and massaging it through the material of his pants. She was turned on by the evidence of his desire and shivered with anticipation as his hardened length continued to grow.

When she was completely naked, he reached out to trace her lines and caress her curves. He followed the shape of her breast with the tips of his fingers and flicked back and forth over her nipple with his thumb. He moved lower and cupped her smooth naked mound, and rubbed delicate circles around her opening before he dipped inside her warmth, seeking telltale evidence that she was wet and ready for him. She welcomed his invasion and held onto his arms for stability, pushing helplessly into his hand as he indulged himself.

When he removed his tormenting finger, he reached behind her and picked up the pair of shorts. He kneeled in front of her and put his arms around her waist. Pulling her closer, he buried his face in her pelvis and inhaled the scent of her arousal. He flicked his tongue repeatedly, delving into her divide to taste her spice. She moaned, nearly lost her balance, and held on tighter. Again he withdrew and temporarily halted his torture and lowered the shorts to the floor, encouraging her to step into them, one leg at a time. They fit her like a glove and molded perfectly to her rounded bottom. Next, he helped her into the harness, lifting her breasts through the openings and pulling it tight, then lacing it up from behind to bring her shoulders back and lift her breasts higher. Before putting on the pasties, he suckled each nipple, licking, nipping and teasing them to pointed perfection. And last, he helped her put on the heels and watched her height increase and bring her to a level only a few inches shorter than his six feet plus.

His tantalizing tease changed from gentle and coaxing to dark and demanding; his gaze became hard and possessive. Suddenly he bent his knees and lifted her up. Putting her over his shoulder like a prehistoric caveman, he headed off down the hallway to his bedroom. He put her down in the middle of the floor and held her captive in his arms. Candace viewed her surroundings through wide-open eyes. She was always impressed by the heavy, dark-stained oak king bed prominently displayed in the middle of the room. The headboard was covered with black leather held in place by rounded bronze tacking pins. In the middle was the sculptured bronze head of a lion, pressed flush against the board, with a small metal hoop that hung between its teeth. It was a beautiful piece of workmanship. Whenever she looked at the bed, she couldn't help but see a reflection of the man with its masculine beauty and implied strength.

Placed next to the bed was a small serving table that held an assortment of items: crystal goblets, an ice bucket, a bottle of champagne, a bowl of fruit, chocolate sauce, whipped cream— and nipple clamps.

Chapter 22

"I want you to close your eyes and open your mind, Candace." He spoke into her ear as he wrapped his arms around her body from behind and pulled her back against his chest. "I want you to *feel* what it is I feel for you." He took her hand and placed it between his legs, encouraging her to wrap her fingers around his engorged length, to stroke and grip it firmly. "I want you to know what it is you do to me every time you're near me and every time I think about you." He withdrew a long black silk scarf from his back pocket and let it trail over her skin, through her fingers, up her arm, around her neck, and over her face.

"Since this is our first time experimenting together like this, we're going to take it slow," he whispered into her neck and nipped at her shoulder. "I want you to trust me and believe I would never hurt you. This night is about pleasure, for the both of us. Do you believe me, Candace?"

This time she didn't hesitate. "Yes. I believe you, Brice."

"That's my girl." He placed the scarf over her eyes and tied it behind her head. Then he turned her around to face him.

"Kiss me," he commanded. And she did, wrapping her arms around his neck and putting every ounce of excitement and fear she felt into it, signaling her surrender and leap of faith. The kiss went on forever, tongues battling, hearts pounding, and internal temperatures escalating toward meltdown. She wrapped one leg around his lower body, bringing her center snug against his enormous hard-on. He pressed his cock against her latex-covered pelvis and ground his hips back and forth. The friction of his jeans rubbing against the zipper in her shorts directly over her sensitive button was an excruciating, painful pleasure. She moaned in submission and felt her knees weaken from the pressure as she approached orgasm.

"Oh no you don't," he scolded as he pulled back from her embrace. "It's not going to be *that* easy. You took your sweet-ass time letting me back into your space. I think you enjoyed making me wait and beg to see you. But there's something you should know about me, Candace. I'm not accustomed to waiting or begging for what I want."

He pulled her close again and bent forward to lick her lips and trace wet kisses along her cheek. Nipping at the soft shell of her ear, he whispered low and passionately, "You made me think about your hot delicious body day and night, and all the things I wanted to do to you. How I wanted to please you, how I wanted you to please me. Now it's your turn to endure the agony of anticipation. We're going to do things my way tonight. I think you should know what never-ending need feels like."

The hard pressure of his cock and the husky sound of his voice sent waves of heat cascading down her spine. He took her hands and clasped them together in front of her. "I want you to undress me. Use your senses to feel me and touch me while you take my clothes off." He released his grip and enjoyed the sensation of her soft exploring hands moving methodically over his frame.

The blindfold was something new, something exciting. It quieted her nerves and heightened her senses, making her more conscious of the muscled form beneath her fingertips. She concentrated on the sensations conveyed by her sense of touch. Sliding her hands under his shirt, her fingers traced every line and every defined detail as she rubbed her palms over his skin and raked her fingernails across his now rigid nipples. She lifted his shirt, pulled it slowly over his arms and head, and dropped it to the floor, then rubbed her face over his chest and abs as she worked her way down his torso. She tasted and teased him with her tongue and fingers, while slowly moving lower.

His thighs were like two strong tree trunks, hard and immovable. She lowered herself to her knees and fit her body between them. With hands holding onto his firm butt, she rubbed her face against the bulge of his still-covered cock, relishing in the feeling and scent of him. Next, she turned her attention to his boots, unsnapping and removing and tossing them aside. From her kneeling position, she gripped the zipper and slid it down and over the swollen bump in his pants. As she eased his pants down past his buttocks and strong thighs, her breath hitched when she came into contact with a soft leather thong pulled taut, cupping his manhood and leaving his backside bare to her exploring touch. Her excitement went up another notch.

Too soon he pulled her up by her elbows and deprived her of the pleasure of worshiping his masculine form. He wrapped a second scarf around her wrists and tied her hands together in front of her. He laid her on the bed and looped the loose end of the scarf through the hoop in the lion's mouth, pulling her arms high over her head and tying it in place.

"How do you feel, Candace?"

"Nervous," she whispered.

"It's okay, baby." He nuzzled her neck and softly traced lingering kisses along her collarbone, down her throat, and onto the top of her breasts. "You can be nervous for now," he murmured, "but I promise you, it won't last. The scarf isn't tight. You can get out of it anytime you want, if you're afraid or feel uncomfortable."

He took an ice cube from the bucket, pressed it to her mouth, and brushed it back and forth over her tempting, protruding bottom lip. He leisurely licked away the drops of water left behind, then explored the seam of her mouth with his tongue, seeking entrance, coaxing her to open for him. The fiery warmth from his aggressive, probing tongue caused her to quiver and made her wet. He ended the kiss and then gradually peeled back one of the pasties from her breast and covered it with his lips, again scorching her with the heat from his tongue. Sucking it hard against the roof of his mouth, it transformed into a tight hard peak, and he grazed it with his teeth and bit down upon it gently. She moaned her pleasure.

He removed his mouth from her breast, pinching and rolling her nipple between his thumb and forefinger. Then he replaced his fingers with his now-cold wet tongue, rolling the ice cube over her nipple and across her breast.

The sensation was intense. Her senses were shocked by the instant change in temperature, from intensely hot to icy cold. He took the cube and rolled it over both her hardened buds until they were numb with cold, then he attached the soft rubber-coated nipple clamps with adjustable screws and a connecting chain that ran between the two clips. He turned the screws to adjust the tension to her level of tolerance. The sudden pinch of pain instantly turned into an intense blooming pleasure.

He returned to ravaging her body with his ice-cold mouth, licking her inside her navel and rubbing her everywhere with his face. The sensation was nearly unbearable. Unexpectedly, he grasped her hips and clamped down hard, spread her legs, and pushed his face between her thighs. Toying with the zipper tab at the seam of her shorts with his teeth, he gradually pulled it down to reveal the treasure underneath. He stuck his cold, cold tongue on her clit, circled it twice, and plunged deep inside. She gripped the tied end of the scarf with both hands, let out a scream, and nearly jumped off of the bed.

It wasn't like anything she'd ever felt before. A tingling sensation streaked up her torso and down through her legs, straight to the end of her toes. Her entire body shook uncontrollably. With an audible growl, he draped her legs over his shoulders, lifted her higher, and pushed his face in further between her legs. He continued his assault until the heat from her core melted the ice cube completely. Then he traveled back up her body to once again feast on her lips.

He took another ice cube and applied it to her nips, keeping them numb. He brushed a fresh, ripe strawberry covered in chocolate across her lips then popped it into her mouth. She sucked and chewed on it.

"Are you okay, Candace? Do you want me to stop?" he asked as he nuzzled her throat and toyed with her earlobe. "Tell me if it's too much."

"No, no, no," she stammered. "Don't stop." The painful pleasure that spread through her body, delivered by the ice and the pinching clamps, was a new and shocking experience. She wasn't ready for it to end. Not yet.

• • •

Her willingness to take part in his type of foreplay excited him. The way she'd screamed and quivered beneath his mouth made his cock grow even harder. It had been too long since he'd played his sex games.

He twirled her over and put her face down and on her knees. A large wedge-shaped pillow was placed beneath her stomach and hips to set her ass high, and he loosened the scarf to allow her arms enough slack to rest her weight on her elbows.

"Spread your legs for me, Candy."

He fit his body between her legs and clutched her butt cheeks, one in each hand, then rubbed his leather-clad cock and balls along the open zipper. The heat from her soft, moist flesh was excruciating. Reaching around her body with one hand, he tugged slightly on the chain that joined the clamps on her nipples as he ground his body against her backside. With the other hand, he delivered a stinging slap to one cheek. She let out a loud gasp. He rubbed his hand over her rounded form to take away the sting, and then delivered another quick sharp slap to the opposite cheek. He raked his fingers up her thighs and grabbed her ass again, rocking his weight into her.

He continued to stroke her butt with one hand as he pushed a finger into her moistened depths in search of her sweet spot. He fingerfucked her fast and deep, alternately playing with her clit and tugging on her nipples with his free hand. Then he pulled his cock free from the leather thong and rubbed it against her wet opening. He eased the broad, flared tip of his penis slowly in and pulled it out. The open zipper raked across his cock like the nails of tiny little fingers, and created an incredible sensation that sent whips of electricity streaking over his ass, through his balls, and all the way down to tickle his toes.

"Do you like this, baby?" he growled. Unable to control his body's automatic response, he pushed in further.

"Yes, you know I do," she moaned, the sound of her voice muffled by the bed sheets bunched beneath her face.

"Do you want more of me?"

"Yes, I want more. I want it all." Candace pushed her ass back into him, tugging against her restraint, struggling to press herself closer. Brice pulled back and slapped her butt again. He felt her body tremble from the contact.

"Naughty girl. Not yet. Not until I'm ready. I told you, tonight we're going to do things my way."

He was having difficulty maintaining control. The sight of her lovely ass covered in latex, exposed and propped up high, and the black Christian Louboutin stiletto heels did things to him. The sinuous feel of her slick channel stretched and wrapped around him made him just a little bit crazy. Brice pushed inside of her again, going deeper; he moved in slow, easy in-and-out strokes. Her soft walls gripped him like a silken fist, pulsing and squeezing him tight. He shuddered. She moaned louder and squirmed and rolled her hips more.

"Dammit, Candy—don't move," he rasped. Holding onto his self-control by a thread, he dragged himself back just in the nick of time. His hand fisted around his shaft and gripped it hard while he fought to ride out the waves of sensation. She would *not* do this to him; there was no way he'd allow her to take him over the edge too soon.

"I can't help it," she whined, unsated and frustrated. "You're torturing me."

"Yeah. That's the idea." He breathed heavily. "I spent the last two weeks jerking off in my bed every night, thinking of you just like this—your ass in the air and me buried up to my nuts in this tight pussy of yours." He rubbed his free hand in small circles over her buttocks, then up her spine, his fingers tracing the slightly raised ridge of bone surrounded by taut muscle.

"*That's* torture."

He relaxed his death grip and began to stroke himself in a slow, measured glide, up and down his shaft. Though it momentarily eased the intensity of his urge for release, the clutch of his hand couldn't compare to the feeling of being wrapped in warm, wet, liquid silk. He circled her entrance, dipping inside and pulling back, drawing out his pleasure and adding to her torment. He couldn't help himself. The sensation was agonizing as it sent white-hot heat streaking up his legs to register in his groin. His toes crossed and snapped as though a switch connected to his ass had sent a powerful electrical current surging throughout his body. He was playing with fire, and loving every minute of it. He could barely stave off the wave of heat running rampant from his head to his toes.

He reached underneath her body and simultaneously released the nipple clamps and slammed his pelvis into her, pushing deep, as far as he could get. She let out a shudder, signaling her surprise, or maybe pleasure. He pressed one hand into her back to hold her in place, then gripped her by her hair with the other and held on.

His body was hard and hot; it glistened with sweat as he settled into his rhythm and paced himself for a long ride. He glided into her repeatedly, riding her furiously, then slowing down to catch his breath and fight the powerful compulsion to let go. He brought her to the brink, again and again, taking them to the edge but refusing to go over it, holding her back from release. He wasn't willing to let the feeling end, not yet. Not until he was ready.

"Brice, please."

"Please, what?"

"Please, you have to stop this torment. I want to come. I *need* to come," she moaned in desperation.

"Not just yet, babe. It's going to take me a while to get rid of this build-up. You made me wait too long. You've got a sweet pussy, Candy. It's so sweet that I want to stay locked up and buried deep in it forever. You put me through hell, keeping it from me. I want you to think real hard before you make me wait this long again." He slammed into her with each word, emphasizing his displeasure with being allowed only limited access to her sweet treat. It was a mistake. The harder he pushed and the deeper he drove, the more it intensified the surge of heat that moved through him, and it set him ablaze.

He lost his grip on that last thread of control, and then pure animal instinct took over. He rode her hard, relentless, pumping his hips mindlessly with the speed and power of a pounding jackhammer, driving into her over and over like she was the last piece of ass he would have in this lifetime. She must have sensed his waning resolve and moved to take advantage of his moment of weakness.

Candace loosened the binding scarf and used her hands to brace herself against the onslaught of his continuous pounding. She rose up and pushed back to grind into him, meeting his thrusting hips and driving cock with a matching powerful force of her own. The slapping sound of wet flesh on flesh and growling emissions of uncontrollable grunts and groans echoed throughout the room. And then it happened. Unable to hold back the intense rush of liquid heat, he let go. His release was like a runaway freight train, barreling uncontrollably forward toward an explosive end. The feeling took him over the edge, into darkness and beyond. The roaring sound of Brice's voice filled the air, joined by Candace's own high-pitched keening wail, followed by his complete and utter collapse as every muscle in his body gave out and he fell forward, draping his bulk over her.

Chapter 23

"I'm sorry, babe. I think things got a little out of hand." He grinned at her and lifted her gold-and-silver braided anklet to show it had snapped into two pieces. "I might have gotten a little carried away. But don't worry." He laid it on the nightstand and then placed a string of kisses across the top of her foot, working his way up to the now bare spot left by the missing piece of jewelry. "I know you never take it off, so I'll have it fixed and back on this pretty little ankle of yours before you know it."

"Honey, right now, a snapped ankle chain is the last thing on my mind." She rewarded him with tinkling laughter as she pulled him up to cuddle him in her arms.

He covered her body like a blanket, buried his face in her neck, and squeezed her hard. He was suddenly overcome with a strong and inexplicable emotion. His mouth felt dry, and his heart started to pound. He wanted to hold her like this forever. His grip tightened, and she squeezed him back.

"Brice, baby, are you alright?"

He waited for the moment to pass, then gave her a quick peck on the forehead before rolling over to grab his nearby jeans. "Yeah, sure I am. Are you hungry? I'm starved. Come on, let's get something to eat. Keeping you satisfied is a full-time job, and I need sustenance to keep my strength up." The words tumbled all over one another as he hurried to cover the rush of unexpected feelings.

"I'd love to, but I'm so exhausted I don't think I can even walk. Besides, I have nothing to wear; all of my clothes are in the other room."

There was a mischievous lilt in her voice as she sat up and leaned against him, her head over his shoulder and her bare breasts pressed into his back. Circling his waist from behind, she brushed playful fingers over his limp manhood. "We both know I don't mind walking around buck-ass naked. But I know how excited you get when you see me without any clothes on." She laughed in his ear. Brice groaned as he bent over and rummaged through a drawer and pulled out a pajama top.

The musical tinkle of her voice and the light stroke of her hands on his cock stirred more than the usual physical response. He was moved much deeper inside. She was right; he loved watching her nude body, and whether in motion or standing still, it never failed to arouse him. He also loved seeing her dressed in only his nightshirts. It gave him a sense of pride and possession to have her wrapped in silk and covered in his scent.

"Here." He tossed her the shirt. "Wear this." He pulled on his jeans. "And these." He grinned as he leaned down to pick up the black stiletto pumps and dangled them from the tips of his fingers. She eyed the shoes with a wicked grin of her own and extended her hand. As he watched her slip into the shirt and heels, the sight of her made him instantly hard all over again. But instead of pushing her onto the bed and striping her bare, he hoisted her onto his back and carried her piggyback to the kitchen—relishing the soft silk sliding over his bare skin, the sight of brown legs and black pumps wrapped around his waist, and the sound of her delighted giggles reverberating in his ear.

• • •

Lounging together in bed, nestled among plumped-up pillows and tangled sheets, they feasted on strawberries dipped in chocolate sauce and indulged in tall glasses of chilled champagne. Brice was secretly amazed to find himself enjoying every second. He'd spent most of his life avoiding intimacy like this, never wanting to get this close, to be this exposed. With Candace, it was different.

It felt right, like the most natural thing in the world. Caught up in the miracle of this woman and the moment, he knew he'd never be able to go back to a life devoid of this feeling. He pondered his growing, intimate desire to know everything there was to know about her.

Candace noticed him staring at her intently, and she frowned. The laughter they'd shared with such ease had faded away, replaced by an unusual and still silence. "You have a serious look on your face, babe." She traced her finger over the deepened crease that extended from brow to brow and gazed into his eyes. "What's on your mind?"

Instead of answering, Brice threaded his fingers in her hair and watched in silent wonder how the curls seemed to come alive, to coil and snake around his hand and wrist as if to hold him captive.

The image resurrected pieces of his fantasy dream and suddenly made him want to believe in mythical creatures with magical gifts. She was a witch, an enchanted being of infinite power who'd entangled him with her spell and changed his life forever. She'd wrapped herself around his body and his heart so tight he knew he'd never be free. He didn't want to. In that instant, he realized the last vestiges of his uncertainty had vanished. He finally knew where he was headed and what he wanted in life. He wanted her. She was the one. And the revelation warmed him inside and lifted his soul.

A reminder of that long-ago conversation with David flashed in his head. He remembered proclaiming his refusal to become part of the "brotherhood of the fallen." But that was before. Now, he couldn't fathom living in a world without Candace. Things had changed since he'd agreed to go along with her proposal. He'd had his doubts all along, but now he knew for certain he'd never be satisfied with the limitations imposed by such an agreement. All he had to do was to persuade her that he was what she needed in her life. He was convinced the situation had altered for her too, that she was just too stubborn to admit it.

"Nothing much, I was just wondering."

"Wondering, about what?"

"I was wondering, why is it you're so dead set against a regular relationship?" He drew her face closer and gently brushed his thumb across her cheek. "I know you told me that you're not interested in an exclusive one-on-one arrangement, especially with a nice guy." He stopped stroking her cheek momentarily and gave her a faint smile. "But I can't help but think there's more to it than that. What's the real story, Candace? Who broke your heart and kept you from trusting other men? I want to know what bastard stole your faith in love and messed things up for a guy like me. Tell me, because I really want to know." *I need to know.*

• • •

His question took her completely by surprise. She'd never in her wildest dreams expected to engage in a heart-to-heart conversation with Brice, or any man. Men didn't talk about love and heartbreak. Every woman knew their favorite conversations revolved around beer, boobs, and bitches, and probably in that order. She didn't know what to say. She stiffened, sat up, and gradually pulled away from his grasp, suddenly needing to create distance between them. "It was a long time ago," she finally answered in a quiet voice.

"Not so long ago if it still haunts you, and has power over you. What happened, Candace?"

Candace clasped her hands together in her lap and studied them with downcast eyes. She didn't want to have this conversation, but Brice wasn't the kind of guy to be put off when he wanted answers. He was persistent and steady, two things she admired about him most.

How much should she tell him? Part of her wanted to simply let go and spill everything, and share every hurt and disappointment she'd ever had. But another part warned she'd be a fool to give him that kind of power, to leave herself vulnerable to criticism and judgment. So she hesitated, too afraid to open up and expose her pain. Though years had passed since her heart had been broken, the hurt and humiliation was as raw and fresh as if it had happened yesterday.

"I don't want to talk about it."

"You can trust me, Candace. After all we've shared, I want you to feel like you can tell me anything." He stared at her with searching eyes.

"It's not that, Brice."

"Then, what is it?"

There it was. That persistent persona she both respected and shrank away from. *Why can't he just let it go?*

"I don't want to dredge up old hurts and open old wounds. It took a long time to put it behind me, and if you don't mind, that's exactly where I'd like to leave it." It wasn't that she didn't trust him with her past. She didn't want to trust him with her future.

"I don't understand. Was being in love such a bad experience? Weren't there good times too, at least enough to give it another shot?"

She pulled her knees up into her chest and wrapped her arms around her legs. She tried to sound relaxed and unaffected by his questions.

"Sure, there were 'good times,' but the good didn't outweigh the bad. It was pretty much a one-sided affair. I was in love. He was in lust. It wasn't exactly the ideal combination for your standard happily-ever-after scenario. And yes, I did 'give it another shot.' It was the second time around that made me realize I'm not supposed to have anyone permanent in my life. I'm not a 'three strikes you're out' kind of girl, Brice. It only takes me a couple of times to learn a lesson, and believe me, having my heart ripped to pieces twice was enough to get the point across."

"Is that why you came up with this plan to engage in emotionless and detached affairs? Do you really think it will keep you safe from falling in love again?"

"Yes. Considering the type of men I usually date, that's exactly what I think."

Despite her best efforts, her temper was starting to rise. She didn't like where this conversation was headed. "Why are you asking so many questions, Brice? What do you know about love? Have you ever been in love before?"

"No, I haven't," he replied calmly.

"I didn't think so. You're as guilty as I am when it comes to avoiding relationships that could lead to a long-term commitment. At least I have a reason. What's your excuse?"

"I don't have an excuse. It's just never happened for me before, that's all. I'll admit I haven't gone out of my way to encourage it, but nothing has ever led me in that direction. No sparks. No fire."

"You're saying that in all these years, you've never, not once in your entire life, been in love? Not even a little?"

"No, not even a little. Not even when I was in school. Of course like every teenage boy I chased after girls, and had your typical crushes, but that had more to do with hormones than the heart. Later, when the girls became women, the chase became different, but I never stuck around long enough for things to get complicated. I wasn't any good at pretending to feel something that wasn't there, and I'd be an asshole to lead a woman into believing otherwise."

"Really?" Her voice was heavy with mocking sarcasm. "Were these women aware of this noble gesture on your part, or did you pull a vanishing act and leave them to figure it out on their own?" Sarcasm slowly turned to anger. "Men are such cowards. They don't have the balls to stand in front of a woman and tell her, face to face, they've lost interest and are ready to move on. We're either left in the dark with a lot of unanswered questions—wondering what the hell happened—or baffled by bullshit explanations that would sound more believable coming from a ten-year-old child."

Brice cocked his head to one side and gave her a look that revealed a sudden, dawning understanding. She dropped her eyes to avoid his penetrating gaze, knowing she'd said too much and he saw too deep.

"Things don't work that way for me, Candace. I may be guilty of having a commitment phobia, but that's all. I have nothing but the deepest respect for women, and I've never intentionally hurt or misled anyone. Unlike those other guys you seem familiar with, I'm not afraid to face consequences. When I make up my mind about something, I'm an all-in kind of guy. You should know this about me by now."

A flash of anger tinted her cheeks with a faint crimson blush.

"Are you chastising me?"

"No. I'm educating you. I think it's time you knew who you're dealing with. You need to put aside your preconceived ideas about men in general, and have a little more faith in *this* man."

Candace crossed her arms and gave him a studied look. The seriousness of his expression brooked no argument. Brice was clearly laying down a challenge. She stared back into those unflinching eyes, and her stomach knotted with mounting fear. In that moment, she realized he was telling her that things had changed. He'd moved beyond their limiting arrangement, and he wouldn't be satisfied anymore with the way things were.

"Some things are easier said than done, Brice. Maybe you've never been in love before, but I have, and it hurts like hell. It's a powerful, debilitating emotion that rips you apart and tears you up inside. If you haven't had the pleasure, then I highly recommend you avoid it at all cost." Candace got out of bed and crossed the floor to escape into the bathroom, and closed the door silently behind her.

• • •

Brice gradually awoke as dim morning sunlight filtered into his bedroom. A lazy smile played across his lips as memories of the night before ran through his head. Her natural scent mixed with perfume clung to the pillow beneath his head. He pushed his face in further to inhale the smell, and draw her essence in deeper. His body stirred with arousal. With eyes still closed, he reached out blindly to pull her close, only to find he was grasping at empty space. He opened his eyes and sat up quickly. Candace was nowhere to be seen. He'd pushed her too far, and she'd left sometime during the night.

His prying questions had made her angry. He'd followed her into the bathroom and done his best to soothe her ruffled feathers, but obviously he hadn't done a very good job. She'd come back to bed with him, but she must have been angrier than he'd realized to pick up and leave in the middle of the night. But he stood by his declaration and his challenge. Maybe he was moving too fast and pushing too hard, but he didn't want to wait any longer. It was time she opened her eyes and saw him for who he was—an individual—not someone to be judged by or compared to the miscreants from her past. He'd already proven he was an honorable man. A better man. He deserved her trust.

Brice fell back onto his pillow and stared at the ceiling. His brief moment of happiness had given way to a surprising and profound ache. It was true; he'd never been in love. He'd never experienced this feeling of exploring, reaching, and trying to hold onto something new, or the dull throbbing ache of loss. If this was what it felt like to be denied what your heart desired most, then she was right. Being in love sucked.

Chapter 24

Candace sat on the edge of the mattress with her elbow on her knee, resting her face in the palm of one hand while the other nervously made a twisted mess of the bedcovers. Once again, she'd ignored her instincts and ended up exactly where she always did: right in the middle of a mess. A feeling of impending doom hung over her head like a dark cloud.

It's your own damn fault. She'd allowed herself to be reeled in by his charm and good-guy routine, had become too comfortable with how good it felt to be held in his arms. She'd dropped her guard, losing her inhibitions *and* her mind in the process. His good deeds aside, he'd managed to slide past her defenses one kiss and one awesome sexual adventure at a time. Now he'd taken up residence in a place closer than she'd like, and it scared the crap out of her.

Last night had brought about a change. She wasn't stupid. She couldn't pretend to ignore the reason behind his probing questions. Brice had made a statement loud and clear. So, she'd done the next best thing. She panicked and ran. It was cowardly of her to tuck her tail and run before morning, but it was better that way. She needed time. There was no way to think clearly when she was close to him.

Their night together had been the single most amazing experience in her life—and she wanted more. But she was terrified of what wanting "more" would mean. Candace buried her face in both hands and groaned in frustration.

She got up and headed to the kitchen. Her head throbbed under the weight of her thoughts, and the grumbling ache of hunger in her stomach was growing too loud to ignore. She was rummaging through the kitchen cupboards for something to eat when the phone rang and the doorbell sounded simultaneously. She grabbed the phone while moving forward to answer the door.

"Good morning, babe." She heard the smile in Brice's voice, and the familiar sound brought an immediate sense of peace to her chaotic mind. Despite her earlier misgivings, she couldn't help the glow she felt inside at the mere sound of his voice. She shook her head. *God, I'm a walking contradiction.*

"Good morning back at you."

"I was disappointed when I woke up this morning and found you MIA. You left without even saying goodbye."

"I know, and I'm sorry about that, but you looked so peaceful I didn't want to wake you. I left because it's Saturday, you know, my errand day. I have a lot to do, and I wanted to get an early start." It wasn't a complete lie, but it sounded like a pretty lame excuse even to her ears.

"I wanted to make sure you made it home okay. How are you feeling? Any sore muscles that need attending to?" His voice took on that sexy, wicked tone she loved to hear. "I'd intended to give you a full body massage, complete with warm oils, hot towels, and me."

She laughed. "I'm fine, Brice. As a matter of fact, I'm better than fine. I feel great." The thought of his big, strong hands kneading her muscles and cupping her body filled her head with intimate images of where his massages would ultimately take them. "I'm glad you called. I wanted to thank you for a wonderful evening. I really, *really* enjoyed it."

When she opened the door, waiting there was a UPS guy with a package in his hand. She smiled, signed the receipt, and shut the door. She stared at the small lightweight box in confusion, certain she hadn't ordered anything. The return address was unfamiliar. She continued talking to Brice while she opened the box. As she tore into it, a sheet of paper fell out and landed on the floor. The word WHORE was spelled in cut-out magazine letters glued to the blank page. Inside was a clear plastic baggie that contained the shredded remains of a chocolate-colored lace bra and panty set, one she immediately recognized as her own. A chill went down her spine, and a soft frightened sound escaped her throat.

"Candace? What's wrong?"

"Oh my God." Her voice was scarcely above a whisper.

"Candace! Tell me what's wrong," Brice practically shouted into the phone.

"There's a package. It has my underwear in it, ripped to pieces."

"I'm on my way. Don't do anything, just wait for me." There was silence. "Candace?"

"Okay," she answered and quietly hung up the phone.

While she waited, a hundred questions raced through her head, but she kept coming back to the same two: *who* and *why*. Suddenly, comprehension dawned and the answer was there, glaringly obvious. The over-the-top phone call, the crazy encounter at the restaurant, the break-in, and now this, her underwear in the mail. She suddenly heard the taunting sound of his voice in her head. *"I can find out anything I want to know about you, Freak: your number, where you live, who your friends are—even who you sleep with."* Her heart thudded against her chest, and her stomach turned over. How could she have been so naïve? So stupid? Brice had been right all along. It was Andrew Nash. It had to be. He'd broken into her house, and *he'd* sent the package.

• • •

Brice must have broken every speed limit and traffic law known to man, because he was at her door in well under the forty minutes it usually took to cover the distance. She greeted him with a cup of coffee in one hand and the offending item in the other. To his surprise, she was not the crumpled vision of anguish and tears he'd imagined and expected to see during his drive over. To the contrary, she looked royally pissed. And it was a side of her he'd never seen before.

"Would you like a cup of coffee?"

"Yeah, sure," he said, wary of her calm behavior.

"Have a seat, I'll be right back."

"Are you okay, Candace?" he called as she headed toward the kitchen. "You seem—changed, since we talked."

"I'm fine." A distinct bite of anger tinged her voice as she returned and handed him a cup of coffee. She leaned against the kitchen counter and watched as he gingerly sipped the liquid to test the heat.

"I did some thinking while I waited for you. I remembered what you said on the night of the break-in: how it didn't make sense for a burglar to ransack my house, destroy my things, take nothing, and leave such a personal message behind—to do all those things to a complete stranger. And now, I get this in the mail." She threw the plastic baggie with the torn underwear onto the sofa next to him. "I didn't believe you because it seemed absurd. But the phone call, the run-in at the restaurant, the break-in, and now this. You were right. This is Nash, isn't it?"

Brice looked at the shredded remains of her underwear, and felt a familiar boiling and unfettered anger rise up inside of him.

"Yeah. I'd bet my last dollar on it. Everything points to him."

"Why? Why would he do something like this? What could he possibly hope to gain from all of this crazy stuff?"

"Fear. Intimidation. A sense of power. He's sending you a message."

"What kind of message?"

Brice set his cup aside and stood up, and started pacing the floor. She could feel his anger rolling off of him in waves.

"Sit down, Candace. I have something to tell you, and I want you to hear me out before you say anything." He looked at her with frosty eyes and didn't speak until she'd done as he'd told her. "I took matters into my own hands and hired a private investigator. I did it the same night of the vandalism because I had a gut feeling, and I always go with my gut. You may not like it, but I did what I had to do, and I'd do it again."

He took a calming breath. "You may as well know right now that there are no limits to what I will do when it comes to your safety, and my peace of mind. You're important to me, and I take care of what's important to me."

With that said, Brice admitted everything he'd done up to that point. He told her about the private investigator, Nash's history of harassing and intimidating women, and the telephone cell tower information that proved he was nearby on the night of the break-in. Brice told her he intended to use the information to give Nash a taste of his own medicine, and finished with telling her about Nash's personality profile. "Nash is medically diagnosed with narcissistic personality disorder. When you add in a dose of possible schizophrenic paranoia, what you have is one mentally fucked up dude."

Candace remained quiet for a long while, staring at Brice. The silence made him uneasy.

"Well, Candace, what do you think?"

"I was wondering how in the hell I got myself mixed up in this mess. And I was thinking you must be wondering the same thing, too. Am I right? Are you wondering what kind of woman ends up with a man like Andrew Nash?" Her posture was as rigid as a steel pole. Her eyes flashed in fiery defiance, and there was a hint of self-recrimination in her voice. Brice was taken aback by her anger and hostility, until he suddenly realized she thought she'd brought this all on herself.

"Hold up. Wait a minute. Do you think I blame you for what that asshole has done? Didn't you hear what I said? You're not the only woman he's harassed. Baby, you can't blame yourself for what that idiot does. He's a sick fuck that's been left loose in the world too long, impersonating a normal human being. You had no way of knowing he was a nutcase. It's not as though he had a sign painted across his forehead saying 'Caution, Crazy Fuck Ahead.'"

"I should have known. Lord knows there were enough signs that something wasn't right about him. But I ignored them."

"So, why did you—ignore the signs?"

• • •

Candace closed her eyes and breathed a small sigh of resignation. It was a valid question, one she'd already asked herself a number of times. But she refused to feel ashamed or apologetic for what she'd done. She'd had her reasons for dating him. She'd followed a plan, with a set of rules that guaranteed no chance of commitment, no locals, and no sweet, nice guys. He lived an airplane flight away, and there was nothing even remotely "sweet" or "nice" about him. He fit the profile.

But ever since she'd met Brice, she'd deviated from her strategy and had broken nearly every one of her rules. She shouldn't have messed with the plan. She should have stuck with the assholes. When she spoke, her tone was matter-of-fact.

"We didn't spend a lot of time together, and there were no 'let's get to know each other better' conversations between us. He wasn't communicative, and neither was I. The attraction was purely physical, and at the time that was all that mattered. It was enough. More would have made things complicated. As I said, as a rule I don't do nice." She shrugged. "But I don't do bat-shit crazy either."

Brice's eyes roved over her face, and he pinned her with that familiar cold stare, his features seemingly carved in stone. When he was like this, he made her nervous because she couldn't tell what he was thinking. And though his expression gave nothing away, she felt the weight of that stare down to her bones. It felt like judgment. For an unknown reason, it hurt. She raised her head high and squared her shoulders and waited.

"Are you going to call the police?" he asked.

"No. What would be the point? He's no fool. If he didn't leave behind one fingerprint in an entire house, you can be certain he didn't leave anything on that package. To be honest, I don't know what to do." She lifted her chin and returned his stony stare. "Do you think he's dangerous? Or is this just part of some whacked-out game to scare me because he's pissed off?"

"I don't know, Candace. There's no way of knowing what's going on in that head of his. If you want my opinion, then yes, I think he's dangerous. Trashing your house and sending shredded underwear in the mail reads like something straight out of a psycho crime novel. He may be doing these things just to fuck with your head, and maybe that's as far as he'll go. But I'm not willing to take that chance."

• • •

Her stiff posture and defiant expression set off alarm bells shrieking in his head. They were a warning. She wasn't convinced that he didn't give a damn about how she'd ended up with Nash in the first place. She'd been in flight mode when she left his bed earlier that morning, and this sudden turn of events had only made matters worse. She was running away from what was happening with the two of them, and she would use Nash to drive the wedge in further.

He was dammed tired of Andrew Nash's intrusions. He'd come between them as surely as if he were standing in the same room, and his presence added to the feeling of distrust that hung heavy in the air. *And yes—it's a fucking relationship, whether she wants to acknowledge it or not.*

"I'm going to contact my guy Rick and have him post a closer watch. We don't want him popping up unexpectedly."

It was time to call Blaine. Nash had gone too far, and it was time to push back. This last stunt was psychotic, plain and simple. If what Rick suspected was true, he was already preparing his next move. Whatever it was, it was guaranteed to be something far more dramatic. He'd preyed and fed on the fear of others for so long that he'd grown bold. It was time he had the wind knocked out of him.

Chapter 25

"We lost him," Rick said.

"What do you mean you *lost* him?" Brice was livid.

"He's dropped off the grid. It appears he's been conducting counter surveillance tactics of his own. He must have picked up on one of my guys, got suspicious, and went underground. With his background in evasion techniques, if he's gotten a whiff of a tail, it'll be damn near impossible to reacquire him."

"I want him found, Rick. He's upped his game plan. He sent Candace a pair of her own underwear, ripped up, in the mail. He's taunting her and trying to frighten her, and I won't stand for it. The man is a psychopath, and I don't want him anywhere near her."

"Understood."

• • •

Brice placed a small black-and-gold gift bag on the table and pushed it toward Candace.

She peered inside and took out a long, black velvet box, opening it to find a gorgeous bracelet.

"It's really thoughtful of you Brice, but I can't accept this."

"Why not? Does it break some unspoken rule in our agreement?" There was a small bite to his voice, annoyance that she was so quick to turn down his gift.

"As a matter of fact, yes, it does. This wasn't part of our arrangement."

"Correct me if I'm wrong, but I don't believe our 'arrangement' ever addressed it. So, technically, there's no breach. Besides, before you get all bent out of shape, it's more than just a gift. It's a precaution."

"A precaution? What does that mean?"

"It means we can't take any chances with Nash on the loose. My guy lost him about a week ago, and we don't know where he is. We both think he might be headed this way. When I dropped your anklet off to the jeweler for repair, I came up with an idea. I bought this for two reasons. One, I wanted to buy you something nice, a gift from me, and two, it might come in handy should we need a backup plan. It was custom made to match your anklet, and I had Rick fit it with a GPS tracking device. Should it become necessary, it can be activated and I can find you over a distance. I hope you'll wear it at all times, starting now."

Candace held it up to the light and studied the intricate design. Brice had paid attention to detail. It was an exact replica of her ankle bracelet, made of several fine links of chain mesh, silver, and gold entwined together into a braided length. There were three little gold hearts spaced out over the length of it.

"It's beautiful. But don't you think this is going a little overboard?"

"No, I don't. Nash's behavior is textbook erratic. His past activities show a pattern of escalation after each incident, and the lack of repercussions has made him reckless. He's played these kinds of games for so long he believes he's unbeatable." Brice paused for a moment. "According to Rick, in his current state of mind the logical progression could be an attempted abduction. Because anything is possible, I want you to be prepared. Nash has always been an asshole, but now he's a dangerous asshole."

"Has he ever done anything like that before?"

"No. Not that we know of."

"Then what makes you so sure he'd do something so out there now? Kidnapping is a serious offense. He could go to jail for a very long time."

"We're not dealing with a rational person here, Candace. He crossed the line when he sent you that package in the mail. Rick

152

and I think he's more fixated with you than he's ever been with anyone else, and he's angry. In his mind, you must represent a failure of some sort. Like a mark on his record. You're a strong woman, something he's never encountered before, and he's determined to break you. He needs to prove to himself, and you, that he's stronger than you are. His ego won't allow him to do otherwise."

"Shouldn't we call the police? If he's that dangerous, wouldn't they protect me?"

"And tell them what? The police won't act on allegations alone; they need proof. All we have are suppositions and circumstantial evidence, nothing concrete. We're on our own here, and we have to do what we can to protect ourselves. As long as we expect the unexpected, we're already a step ahead. With Rick's help and expertise, I think we'll be okay."

"This is all so surreal. I'm sorry, but I just can't imagine that Nash would do something that stupid. Harassing calls and vandalism are one thing, but kidnapping? It sounds too farfetched. I'm sure you and Rick know way more about these things than I do, but I still can't wrap my head around the concept." She dropped her head in acceptance as she fastened the bracelet on her wrist. "I guess I'm just going to have to trust you."

"Is that such a bad thing? Haven't I earned your trust, Candace? Have I ever done anything to make you doubt me or my intentions?"

"No. Of course not. I didn't mean anything like that. I meant I'll have to accept that the two of you are more experienced in things like this and you know what you're talking about, that's all."

"Are you sure? Because lately I get the feeling you're pulling away from me. Things have been different ever since the morning you slipped out of bed without saying goodbye. You've barely made time for us. When we are together, you can't look me in the eye, and even worse, you try to pick fights. Are you trying to push me away? We both know something happened that night, that things changed."

"That's the problem, Brice. I don't want things to change. I like our relationship the way it is. Why jeopardize what we have? Why can't we just be friends who happen to enjoy sex together?"

"Sometimes friendship has unexpected consequences," he replied coldly. His jaw tightened and a chill slowly crept into his eyes. "Change is inevitable, Candace. You're an intelligent woman. How could you not know this?"

"Look, Brice, I get it. Maybe you think you're in love. But really, how could you possibly know if you've never been there before? You have nothing to compare this to."

"I know that you matter to me." He took her hand, brought it to his lips, and kissed it lightly as he stared into her eyes. "Besides my mother, no other woman has ever meant more. I'm not a child, Candace. I'm a grown man. I'm no expert, but I know what I feel. And when I'm around you, I feel happier than I've ever been.

"You make me feel excited, interested, captivated, and eager to know everything about you. When we're not together, even for a day, I miss you. I feel an ache. Here." He pressed a hand to his chest. "I get this twisting feeling in the pit of my stomach simply at the thought that I might never see you again. A few months ago, I never imagined such a thing was even possible. I can't lie. The idea of falling in love scares the hell out of me. It's new territory, and the thought of losing everything I am to another person scares me. But the idea of being without you scares me more."

Candace gently pulled her hand from his grasp and clasped her hands together briefly, then nervously fiddled with the bracelet on her wrist.

Brice crossed his arms. "It would seem that we've exchanged places since our first date. If I recall, I was content to settle for average, while you were the adamant thrill-seeker. What happened to that woman who loved the excitement of dancing on the edge and playing with fire?"

"Nothing's happened to her. She's not stupid. She knows her boundaries and doesn't work without a safety net or a fire extinguisher."

"Damn woman, you're a hard nut to crack, but no matter how much you want to avoid the conversation, we are going to talk about this."

"There's nothing to talk about. We had an agreement. No expectations beyond our arrangement. Having a change of heart doesn't negate the agreement."

Brice leaned forward and put his hands on the table. "Am I missing something here? Was this imaginary binding contract ever signed? Because no matter what your mouth is saying, I know I'm not the only one here whose feelings have changed."

"Imaginary or not, changed feelings or not, it doesn't matter. We had an agreement," she doggedly repeated. She was getting irritated. "I knew it. I knew getting involved with you was a mistake from the start. I told you, nice guys always want more." She crossed her arms and gave him an angry scowl. "I should have stuck with the assholes."

"What does that mean? I'm being penalized because I'm a nice guy? Are you saying you *want* to be treated like shit the rest of your life by men like Nash?"

"Yes, maybe I do," she nearly shouted in defiance. "It's what I'm used to, and I'm okay with that."

"That's bullshit, Candace, and you know it. No woman in her right mind wants to be treated that way. You're using your fear of relationships as an excuse."

Brice's own irritation showed as he pinned her with an angry glare. "I'm on to you, Candace Brown, so don't expect me to believe crap like that. I may not have ever been in love before but I've seen the effect a broken heart can have. I know what lengths one will go to avoid more pain. Don't try to feed me bullshit and expect me to swallow it without question. If you want to walk away from this, you're going to have to give me a better reason."

She glared back at him, her eyes filled with fury and brimming with unshed tears, her face flushed. "I don't owe you a 'better reason.' This is my life, and *I* choose how I live it. Don't go on about other people's feelings and act like you know what you're talking about, because believe me, you don't. Standing on the outside looking in doesn't make you an expert. It makes you a spectator. So, forgive me if I question your authority on the subject. You have *no* idea what it takes to get over a broken heart."

"You can rile all you want, but the circumstances remain the same." His voice softened. "Neither of us are experts, but one of us has to have an open mind. Shutting down and refusing to entertain other points of view only makes us both losers. I'm trying to convince you to look beyond the pain. There's a whole other world worth exploring, and I'm asking you to take a chance. I promise you, you won't regret it."

She didn't have to listen to this. Abruptly, Candace started gathering her things—her cell phone, keys, and purse in one hand, and the gift bag in the other. She pushed herself back from the table and stood. "You know what, Brice? It's been a long day, and I'm tired. Would you please take me home?"

• • •

They rode in silence as Brice drove. Candace sat rigidly and stared out the passenger side window, while he stared straight ahead, gripping the steering wheel tightly with both hands. Her anger had receded and given way to defeat and resignation. When they arrived at her place, Brice parked at the curb and shut off the engine, then turned and gave her his full attention.

"This isn't over, Candace." His voice was low and filled with quiet conviction. "You may walk away from me now, but I'm not letting you walk out of my life without a fight. There's too much that's right between us to let it go to waste, just because you're afraid to take a gamble. I don't know what it will take to change your mind, but I'm not giving up until I do."

She touched his chin gingerly with the tips of her fingers and stroked his jawline to soothe the tension and soften his icy stare. Her stubborn resolve had deserted her and left her stranded in a place filled with fear and uncertainty. This man both fascinated and confused her. She wanted to believe him. She wanted to let go of the past and embrace the present, but its hold on her was too tight.

"Who are you, Brice?" she asked, soft and low. "Sometimes when your eyes grow cold and your face turns to stone, I don't know who you are. It scares me and makes me think I'm not good enough ... that I won't measure up to your expectations."

"You know me, Candace. You know me better than you think you do. I don't expect any more from you than I would from myself."

"That's what scares me. You're perfect. I can't live up to perfection." She leaned into him and placed her head on his shoulder. "I'm a mess, and we both know it. I've jumped without looking too many times in my life, with nothing to break my fall. Each time I had to pick myself up and start all over again." Her voice wavered, and she sobbed into his shoulder. "I'm tired, Brice. I'm tired of starting over."

"Babe." He put his arms around her and pulled her in closer. "You're not a mess. You're just afraid, and you have every right to be. But life doesn't come with guarantees; we have to take our chances and let whatever happens happen. All I'm asking is that you let it happen with me. Take a chance on me, Candace. I love you, and I'd never hurt you. This time, if you jump—I promise I'll catch you."

She pulled away from him and gave him a sorrowful look, her eyes brimming with tears and filled with an unfathomable pain. "I can't."

She grabbed up her things, and, clutching her purse to her chest, she got out of the car and practically ran up the walkway to her townhouse.

All her anger had deserted her somewhere between the restaurant and the drive home. In its place were the aching feeling of emptiness and an overwhelming sense of loss. It had taken everything she had in her to walk away from him, telling herself it was for the best. It was a lie. Her heart was breaking, again, and this time it was her own fault. She'd arrogantly believed she was in control, ignored the warning signs, and found out too late that she was in over her head. There was no such thing as being in control. It was an illusion.

She was forced to face the truth and finally admit to herself that she was in love with him, but it didn't matter. How could she love when she was so afraid to fall? She would let him go. It was for the best, because she wasn't strong enough or brave enough to keep him.

With such sorrowful revelations weighing heavy on her heart, Candace pulled off her shoes and crawled into bed. Still wearing her street clothes, she pulled the covers over her head and wept into her pillow.

Chapter 26

"Hey, Brice. This is a surprise," David greeted him warmly as he opened the door. "What brings you to this side of town so late in the evening?"

"I was on my way home when I decided to make a detour. Are you busy? I need to talk."

"No, not really, come on in. Sarona and I were just video chatting."

"Oh, geez man, I'm sorry. I didn't mean to intrude. We can do this another time."

"No, no. It's perfectly fine. We were just about to say goodnight anyway. Come on in and make yourself comfortable, I'll be right back."

Brice entered the house, went straight to the refrigerator, and took out an ice-cold beer, before taking a seat. He hadn't actually planned to stop by. After leaving Candace at her door, he'd driven around aimlessly until he found himself parked in front of David's place. Somehow his car had made its way there completely on autopilot. Even though it was his nature to remain tight-lipped about his personal affairs, something inside of him must have realized he wouldn't get through this on his own.

He'd shamelessly laid himself bare and handed over his heart, giving Candace complete knowledge of the power she wielded over him. And it still hadn't mattered. It wasn't enough.

He needed help. He needed another perspective. David, too, had suddenly fallen in love, so maybe he could offer some advice. It hadn't been easy for him either, but somehow he'd managed to convince Sarona to give him a chance. Brice needed to know his secret.

"So, tell me, man. What's up? Why the long face?" David also grabbed a beer from the fridge and plopped down next to Brice on the sofa.

Brice took a quick drink from his bottle, and then bent forward with his arms draped over his knees. "I'll give it to you straight, so you can get the urge to say 'I told you so' off of your chest. I met a girl and fell in love, but I can't get her to admit that she's in love with me. She's stubborn, unbending, and dead set on ignoring what's happening between us. Basically, I've been beating my head against a stone wall trying to figure out how to change her mind. I'm here because I need some advice. What can you give me?"

David choked on his beer. "Whoa, whoa, whoa. *What?* I'll get to the 'I told you so' in a minute. Right now I need more information. I know I've been living in my own world over the past few months, but I couldn't have missed this much. What have you been keeping from me?"

Brice concentrated on the bottle in his hand, watching the drops of condensation run slowly down the side. He reflected on the first time he'd seen her and recalled exactly how he'd felt in that moment—defiant, defensive, doomed. In a matter of months, everything had changed. He was no longer fighting the feeling or trying to get away from her; he was fighting to hold onto her.

"Her name is Candace, and she's one of a kind. She's beautiful, sexy, funny, smart, and a computer geek, like me. When she speaks, her voice is pure magic. Just the sound of it makes the hair on my body stand up, and it grabs me by the balls and turns me into one big walking hard-on."

"Are we talking about Sarona's friend Candace? She told me you were dating her friend, but I had no idea it was this serious."

"Yeah. It's beyond serious. It's pathetic." Brice downed the last of his beer, and then got up to get another. "I saw it coming, you know. I saw it from a mile away, and there wasn't a damn thing I could do about it. Now, here I am caught in a fucked-up triangle between her, me, and her past. I'm competing against a memory, and I'm losing. Badly."

"What are you saying? She's still in love with someone else?"

"No. It's worse than that. The bastard before me did a number on her. I don't know details because she won't share them with me. What I do know is that he used up the best of her and now there's nothing left. She's broken ... damaged. I want to fix her. I want to pick up the pieces of her heart, put it back together again, and have it beat only for me."

Brice rejoined David and they sat together on the sofa side by side, their feet perched upon the coffee table, staring at the blackened screen of the TV.

"I don't know what to tell you, man. This relationship stuff is all new to me. I'm still feeling my way along. Any advice from me would be like the blind leading the blind."

"Yeah, I know. It was a shot in the dark."

"I think you should get a woman's perspective."

"I thought of that. My only options are her friend Joyce and my mom."

"It probably wouldn't hurt to reach out to both of them. But Joyce knows Candace. She'd have the inside scoop on what makes her tick. According to Sarona, it was Joyce who changed her mind about me. She tipped the scales in my favor, and I will be forever indebted to that woman." David raised his bottle in the air. "I'm in love, and I've never felt so wonderful."

Brice followed suit. "I'm in love, and I've never felt so miserable."

They crossed their bottles at the neck in a toast, and drained them dry.

• • •

She wasn't taking his calls. He'd been trying for a couple of days, but all he was getting was her voice mail and silence. The angry self-righteous bastard in him wanted to show up on her doorstep and bang on the door, to make such a scene that she'd have to open it to save herself from embarrassment. The intellectual in him knew better. He would have to take a more civilized approach.

He'd called Joyce and pleaded with her to intercede. Joyce agreed she would talk to Candace, but told him he needed to give Candace time. He was fast running out of options, but he had one more card in the deck. He needed a more experienced head in the game. It was time to call in the big guns. *Misery is a bitch called love*, he sullenly thought to himself as he punched the familiar numbers into the phone.

"Hi, Mom, how's the trip coming along?"

"Hi, Brice! What a sweet surprise. The trip has been wonderful so far. Traveling the world is so much more fun than being stuck in one place entertaining stuffy, boring old men. I can't believe how much we missed all those years during our official tours."

"Where are you and Dad now?"

"Your father and I are in Uganda making our way south toward South Africa. From there, we're on to New Guinea and Australia."

"I suppose I shouldn't expect the two of you back anytime soon, huh?"

"No dear, we're extending our trip by two months. There's still too much to see and do. Looking in on the old homestead while we're away isn't cramping your style, is it?" She laughed softly.

"No, it's nothing like that. I was only wondering if you two were close to winding down, that's all." There was a short silence on the other end of the line.

"Okay, what's wrong?"

"What do you mean?"

"Brice, I've known you all your life, and a mother knows when there is something wrong with her child. I can hear it in your voice. You didn't call to talk about our trip. So tell me."

He always squirmed under his mother's all-knowing and all-seeing eye. She still had that effect on him, even thousands of miles away. It was almost funny the way she could still make him feel like he was ten years old.

"I met a woman."

"You met a woman?!" She squealed with delight. Brice knew that those four little words conveyed a mountain of meaning to his mother. This was the first time he'd ever spoken about someone he was dating, and it could only mean one thing. He'd finally found "the one." "Oh Brice, you don't know how long I've waited to hear you say those words!"

He laughed at the sound of her enthusiasm.

"Of course I do. As often as you've badgered me with open threats to force me to make you a grandmother before you were too old to enjoy it, believe me mother, I know."

"Well, you can't blame me; you're thirty-five, for God's sake. My grandmother's biological clock is ticking. I want babies, lots of babies to love and spoil and turn into little holy terrors, and then send them home to their parents when I'm done."

"Yes, Mom, I know, but don't start counting babies just yet. The situation is—complicated."

"Sweetheart, it wouldn't be love if it wasn't complicated. What's the problem?"

Brice told his mother everything: the good, the bad, and the troublesome. For the first time in his life, he shared with her his most intimate emotions—and his deepest fear. "She loves me, Mom, I know she does, but she's too afraid to let go of the past. I've tried everything I can think of to get her to change her mind, but so far nothing's worked. I can't get through to her. I was hoping you could tell me what to do."

"Oh, son, it sounds like she's had a bad experience with love. I understand how she must feel. You don't know this, but I was in love with someone else before I met your father. It ended badly for me. I shut down and locked all my feelings away, and vowed I'd never fall in love again. And then your father came along. Believe me, it wasn't easy for him either. It took a lot of time, patience, and perseverance, but I finally came around. These things take time. Unfortunately there's no cure for stubbornness, no pill for instant clarity and understanding. It's something she has to work her way through over time. Don't push too hard, son. You have to be patient."

"I was afraid you'd say that. Her friend told me the same thing. You and I both know patience isn't my strong suit. I would give her anything in the world, Mom. Anything in my power—except time. It's a luxury I can't afford. The longer she has to think about it, the more strikes I'll have stacked against me. Besides, if I know Candace, she's made up her mind and is already making plans to dump me."

"Brice, now that your heart's involved, I have every faith in you that you'll find a way to get through to her. If she's too blind to see what a wonderful, sweet, and caring man you are, then she doesn't deserve you."

Chapter 27

"Well, that's that, another week over and done," Joyce said after seeing off her last clients of the day. "Now all we have to do is log it in the books and sit back and wait to get paid. What do you say to starting the weekend early, kicking off our shoes, and putting our feet up?"

Candace didn't look up from her desk. "I've still got filing to do. I don't want to fall behind."

"Oh come on, Candace. I'm the boss. And the boss says that stuff can wait until next week. We haven't had any time to ourselves for girl talk. I want to catch up and hear all about you and Brice."

Candace reluctantly put aside the piles of paperwork and followed Joyce into her office, where they made themselves comfortable on the sofa. Joyce kicked off her shoes and tucked her feet under her body, offering a cheery smile, while Candace presented a stiff and unresponsive front.

"So, how are things going? I'm curious to know how your 'friends with benefits' arrangement is working out for the two of you."

"You can cut the crap, Joyce. I know Brice called you. If you brought me in here to lecture me, you may as well save your breath. I don't want to hear it. I love you like a sister, but this is none of your business."

"Wow. Am I that transparent? Don't answer that. Okay, so I'm busted. Just hear me out, and then I promise I won't say another word on the subject." She was treading on super-thin ice, but Candace let her continue. "You're right. Brice did call, out of frustration and desperation. You can't blame the poor man. He's never been in love before, so he doesn't have a clue on how to handle the situation. He's trying to figure out what to do with his heart and your pain. He asked me for advice."

"What did you tell him?"

"Nothing he didn't already know. He's not searching for secrets, Candace; he's seeking solutions. I told him that it's been four years since you got out of a bad relationship, and it was high time you got over it. You can be angry all you want, but it's the truth. You've spent the last four years allowing your life to be ruled by your past—by things you had no control over then, and have no control over now. You've cut yourself off from the prospect of having a normal relationship with a good and caring man. Instead of moving forward, you've stood still and endowed that worthless, lying SOB with too much power. It's time for you to get over him and get on with your life."

Candace bowed her head and twisted her hands together in agitation. "I got over the man a long time ago. It's the pain I can't seem to get over."

Joyce reached out and stroked Candace's hands to calm her nerves.

"Honey, I understand your reluctance to trust someone new, but painful experiences are a part of life. Living through them is what makes us stronger and helps us to appreciate the happiness that comes after. You *have* to let go of your past, Candace, because you can't keep letting it rob you of your future. It's served its purpose. It made you step back and hold out for something better, and that's what you've found in Brice—a better man."

"How do I know that, Joyce? How do I know he's a better man? Men tell you what they think you want to hear until they get what they want, and then they move on." She pulled her hands free and wrapped her arms around her middle. Joyce leaned back and gave her a thoughtful look.

"What is it you think Brice wants from you, Candace? It can't be sex. You've already been there and done that. If he's a typical man only after one thing, then why is he still here?"

"I don't know. Maybe he's into collecting trophies. Maybe he gets his kicks from messing with my head. Maybe that good-guy façade is nothing more than an act, and I'm too blind to see through it. It wouldn't be the first time."

"You're being ridiculous, and we both know it. You're determined to turn Brice into a villain so you'll have an excuse to avoid reality."

"What reality is that, Joyce?"

"The one with the man who loves you."

Candace rose from her seat and crossed the room to stare out of the window. "You know what, Joyce? You're absolutely right. There's not a day that goes by that I don't tell myself the same thing. But none of it really matters. My mind is made up; I'm going to end it with Brice. I won't see him anymore."

"That's it? Just like that. You're going to walk away and give up the best thing that's ever happened to you."

"Yes. Just like that."

"Why?"

"Because I'm a coward, and I'm too damned scared to do otherwise."

"What about Nash? Are you going to just ignore him, too? What will you do if he turns up again?"

"I think Brice is overreacting. Nash can't possibly be that stupid. I'm sure he's just trying to scare me with a lot of melodramatic pranks. He's probably sitting at home laughing about how clever he is in making the 'freak' squirm. But whatever happens, I'll deal with him when the time comes. Now, if you'll excuse me, I'm going to take your advice and leave that pile of files for later. I'm taking the rest of the day off."

• • •

Candace walked across the parking lot toward her car, frustrated that Joyce was clearly taking Brice's side in all this. Wasn't she supposed to be *her* friend first? Why did Joyce refuse to listen to her side of things?

"What's up, Freak?" a menacing voice whispered into her ear. "Long time no see." She froze, goose flesh rising on her arms. He stood close, crowding her against the car. "Where's your fucking shadow?"

"What are you doing here?"

"Aww, aren't you happy to see me? I've come all this way to give you another chance to kiss and make up, with no hard feelings. You should be grateful I'm such a good sport. Hell, I'm feeling so generous, I'll even overlook your slutty fling with the poor little rich boy."

Candace turned and stared at Nash, speechless. His handsome face was harsh and twisted, and his eyes glittered with maniacal glee. She didn't even recognize the man in front of her. Suddenly, she was afraid. She slowly backed away to put distance between them, but he grabbed her by the arm and cut off her retreat.

"Look, Freak, I'll cut to the chase. This isn't a social visit. You and I are going for a ride. Get in the car." Her eyes moved from his scornful face to the hand he'd wrapped around her arm. He wore a pair of translucent rubber gloves, and the sight of them frightened her even more.

"You can't be serious. Either you're crazy, or you think I am. There is no way in hell I'm getting in a car with you."

Nash stunned her with a vicious slap across her cheek. "Don't call me crazy. Now get in the goddamn car." She reacted with mindless rage as she rounded on him with an open palm and slapped him back, followed by pummeling fists. Fear was momentarily overridden by fury. Then, abruptly, she set off running, catching him off-guard. Unfortunately he recovered quickly and gave chase, catching her by her hair and jerking her back against him. "Where do you think you're going, bitch?" He brandished a small-caliber pistol in her face. "Scream if you want, but it'll be the last sound you make on this earth."

Candace eyed the weapon warily, but she feared the crazed look in his eyes even more. There'd be no reasoning with a madman. She let him drag her back to the car and, pressing a hand to her burning cheek, started to climb inside on the passenger side.

"No, not there. You're going to drive."

She got behind the steering wheel and followed his instructions, heading across town toward some unknown location. She drove in stunned silence, her mind racing with a dozen escape scenarios throughout the trip; unfortunately, none would get her safely out of the range of a bullet. Approximately forty-five minutes later they reached their destination, a once proud and bustling commercial neighborhood, now an empty and boarded-up shantytown for the derelict and homeless. She parked behind a broken-down van that blended in perfectly with its surroundings.

"Okay, this is it. It's time for you to get out." Before she could so much as lift the door handle, Nash leaned over and jabbed a needle into her upper arm. She yelped at the unexpected prick. Clutching her arm, she glared at him angrily.

"What was that for?"

"It's just a little something to keep you quiet. I don't want any surprises when I'm not looking." As she rubbed the burning spot, he caught sight of her bracelet and roughly grabbed her arm, twisting and turning her wrist to take a closer look. He grabbed the bracelet and twisted the clasp in the process. "What's this, a present from your boyfriend?"

"No." She snatched her arm away. "I've had this since forever."

"You're lying. Take it off."

"Kiss my ass, Nash."

"Don't tempt me." He laughed harshly. "Take it off. Now. Leave everything. Where you're going, you won't need any of this shit. By the time anyone figures out you're missing, it will be too late."

"You're out of your mind if you think you can get away with this."

"What? You think Dudley Do-Right is going to come rushing to your rescue? I don't think he's got it in him. I know his type. He's rich, arrogant, and full of shit."

Candace looked at him with unconcealed rage and contempt. "Don't let the man in the mirror influence your judgment. Just because you're an asshole doesn't mean everyone else is. You may know the type—but you don't know the *man*."

As she spoke the words Candace was struck with a sudden and profound revelation, and her throat grew tight. *Brice.* The image of his face sprang into her head. His square chin, hard jaw, and cold blue eyes. She knew every angle, every line, and every expression. She knew the way his eyes turned to ice when he was deep in thought, and warmed to aquamarine-blue when he held her in his arms or made love to her. She knew the sound of his voice when it rang out with laughter, or took on that mischievous lilt when he leaned in close and whispered in her ear. Everything about him abruptly rushed in and filled her up with love and longing.

She drew in a painful breath as her eyes were opened wide to reality. She finally understood. He'd been telling her the truth all along. He was none of those awful things she'd accused him of. He had never been anything but caring, supportive, and protective: all the things she'd refused to believe in. Her stubbornness had blinded her and made her a fool. She'd pushed him away with her insecurities, and now it was too late. Brice was gone, and she was alone with a crazy man—a crazy man who had taken her bracelet and severed her only link to him.

"Get in the van. It's time to move. That shot is going to kick in pretty soon, and I want to be long gone from here when that happens."

He was right; she was starting to feel woozy and disoriented, and her limbs were getting heavy. Nash grabbed her around her waist and dragged her to the back of the van. Inside were a makeshift mat and pillow, which he deposited her upon before quickly closing the doors. Candace struggled to sit upright, but only managed to prop herself up a little against the side of the van. Her eyelids were closing against her will. As her body slowly surrendered to the effects of the drug, her fear disappeared and was replaced by an absolute faith that, no matter what, Brice would find her. He loved her, and nothing stood in the way of love—not even a madman. When finally her vision blurred and faded to black, the memory of his loving face was the last thing she took with her into the darkness.

Chapter 28

Brice sat at the bar at Chelsea's Bar and Grill with a drink in his hand, watching the mirrored reflections of people as they arrived in groups of two or more. He'd let Blaine talk him into a night out. It should have been the perfect solution to take his mind off of things, but so far it hadn't worked. He still felt miserable.

All he did lately was think about Candace. She filled up all the space in his life—in his dreams and in every waking moment. He couldn't eat, sleep, or breathe without wanting her. The woman had made his life impossible. What had happened to the man he was before he'd met her? He'd lost him somewhere along the way, and now he was sitting in a bar desperately trying to find him at the bottom of a glass.

"I don't know where the hell I put them," Brice muttered as he distractedly searched his pant pockets, dug into his suit jacket, and patted his shirt.

"Put what?" Blaine asked.

"I must have misplaced them somewhere."

"Misplaced what? Man, what the hell are you talking about, your keys?"

"My balls! My goddamn balls! That's what! I haven't seen 'em since the first time she stuck her hands in my pants and pulled them out to play with. And she's been playing with them ever since." He crossed his arms and leaned forward on his elbows. "You know, she used to laugh and call me 'Ice King.' She said I was cool and in control. But that was before she got her hooks into me and started chiseling away, one chip at a time. Now I'm a melted puddle." He picked up his glass and took a healthy swallow. "There was a time when I was the biggest, baddest dog on the block. Now I'm a fucking poodle. I've been castrated."

"Okay, that's enough. You're officially cut off." Blaine reached for his glass and carefully set it aside.

"It's not the alcohol. It's the woman that's making me crazy." Brice pushed the drink further away, propped his elbows on the counter, and dropped his face into his hands. "I've finally found the right woman. A woman I could settle down and make a life with, and she's running like a scared cat in a room full of rocking chairs."

Blaine stared at him in amazement.

"Damn man, I never thought I'd see the day. Your ass is *whipped*."

"You think?"

"Hey, no need to get testy. I'm just saying…it couldn't happen to a nicer guy."

He snickered.

Brice stared straight ahead, his eyes cold and hard. "I'm glad you find my misery so entertaining.

"Nah, man, it's not that. I'm just in a state of shock. Give me a minute."

"It's too bad my real friend is out of pocket, and I'm stuck with your insensitive ass."

Blaine chuckled softly as he scanned the club. His eyes settled on a spot over Brice's shoulder. "*Hello*," he uttered in a low, distracted voice, his eyes bright and sparkling with sudden interest. "Lookie here, lookie here. I haven't seen this one before."

Brice turned to follow his gaze and was surprised to see Joyce threading her way through the crowd, headed in their direction. He watched in fascination as bodies swiveled and heads turned in her wake. She was dressed in a fitted black-and-gray pinstripe suit with a gray low-cut silk blouse underneath. She looked like a supermodel, and the barroom floor was her runway. Witnessing the wolfish reaction of the male population brought out Brice's protective streak.

"Hey, Joyce, how are you? I didn't know you hung out at Chelsea's." Brice greeted her with a hug and a kiss on the cheek. "Blaine Stanford, meet Dr. Joyce Jeffers. Joyce is a friend of Candace's."

"Hello. I'm pleased to meet you." Blaine grinned broadly as he took her hand and shook it lightly. Joyce smiled politely and returned his handshake, then quickly turned her attention back to Brice.

"I've been trying to find you."

"Really? Why didn't you call my cell?"

"I did, but my calls kept going to voice mail. I finally had to call Sarona and have her ask David if he had any idea where you were. He said you were meeting someone here."

Brice pulled out his cell phone and was alarmed to see six missed calls, four from Joyce and two from Rick.

"What's wrong?"

"It's Candace. I can't find her."

"What do you mean you can't find her?"

"I ended my last session early today, so I suggested we take some downtime and enjoy some girl talk. We got into a discussion— well, actually I was meddling, attempting to intervene on your behalf. It didn't go over well, and she basically told me to mind my own business. Afterwards she said she was taking the rest of the day off, and left. I've been calling her ever since to apologize, but she's not answering her phone."

"Well if she was upset, maybe she's just trying to cool off before she talks to you again."

"You don't understand. No matter how upset she may be, Candace would never not answer her phone. I'm her friend, true, but I'm also her boss. Our working relationship is very professional, and the patients' needs take precedence over hurt feelings. She would answer, no matter what. Besides, I went by her place, and her car isn't there. She's been gone for hours, Brice, and I don't know where she is. This isn't like her."

A cold chill crept down his spine. He hastily picked up his phone and accessed his voice mail to hear the missed messages from Rick.

"Brice, this is Rick. I have an update on Andrew Nash. We recently interviewed a few of his coworkers on the pretext of a routine security background check. On the condition of anonymity, a couple of them were pretty outspoken regarding what they really thought of him. One guy in particular, a Samuel Niemeyer, had some interesting feedback that might prove to be significant in locating him. Call me."

Brice listened to the second message.

"Brice, call me, it's important."

"Shit!"

"What? What's wrong?" Joyce asked with a sudden look of fear in her eyes.

"I don't know, but I've got a bad feeling." Brice speed-dialed Rick's number and held up his hand to ward off more questions from Joyce while he waited for an answer.

"Hello? Rick?"

"Brice. I've been trying to reach you."

"Yeah, I know. I just got your messages. What is it you were saying about Nash?"

"Like I said, my guys picked up a lead from a coworker named Samuel Niemeyer. Nash apparently came to him with a story about being stalked by a former lover and needing a place to lay low until he could shake her. Niemeyer says he was leaving town on business and agreed to let Nash stay in his home for a few days. He says when he got back, Nash was gone and had stolen his car. He considered reporting the theft, but the next day he received a notification and traffic fine via mail that it had been picked up from airport parking and towed to impound.

"We searched for plane tickets purchased by Nash and came up empty, but we got lucky passing his photo around at the rental car agencies. A kid at Hertz remembered him, mainly because of his shitty attitude, and said that he rented a car using a different name. He logged his destination as upstate New York. I'm convinced that was a ruse and that he's either on his way to Atlanta or is already here."

Brice listened to Rick with his heart in his throat. This news, coupled with the inability to locate Candace, put a knot in his gut.

"How long ago was this?" His voice was strained.

"He rented the car a little over a week ago. If he drove from New York to Atlanta, then he's probably been in the area for at least a few days."

"Rick, we don't know where Candace is. Joyce hasn't been able to reach her by phone. I need you to activate the device in her bracelet and get me the coordinates—now."

"Sure thing. Stand by."

Brice heard the unmistakable clicking sound of keyboard strokes as he anxiously waited for the information. His mind raced with possibilities, and none of them were reassuring. While he waited, he filled Blaine and Joyce in on the details.

"Got it," Rick finally said.

Brice signaled to Joyce he needed something to write with, and she hurriedly handed him pen and paper.

"Okay. Go ahead."

"According to the GPS system, she's located at the intersection of 25th and Myrtle, which would put her somewhere on the south side of town."

"Thanks, Rick. I want you to stand by, just in case I need backup."

"No problem. I'll be waiting for your call."

Joyce moved aside his hand to look at the location he'd scribbled down. Her brow creased in confusion, and she shook her head.

"What is it, Joyce? I don't like that look."

"Is this where Candace is supposed to be?"

"Yes."

"This doesn't make sense. That's way on the other side of the city. Candace would never go there without a reason."

"How do you know? Maybe something unexpected came up."

"Obviously you know nothing about that part of town. To call it a rough neighborhood would be an understatement. It's run down and virtually controlled by thugs and felons. All the law-abiding citizens who could afford to moved out a long time ago. Trust me; it's not the kind of place any woman would go to alone."

"Joyce, the monitoring equipment Rick uses is state of the art. It's precise. If that's where the reading says she is, then that's where she is. Or at least, that's where the device is. Hopefully, her being out of touch is simply a case of lousy reception, and all of this will just be a bad scare."

"What if it's not just a bad scare?" Blaine asked. "What's your next move?"

"My next move is to hunt the bastard down and beat him to within an inch of his life, or kill him."

"Look man, I've got your back. But I can't stand by and allow my best friend to commit a crime. We need a solid backup plan, something *other* than beating the crap out of the man or committing murder. I know people in law enforcement, and the district attorney is a close friend. If by chance we need to call officials in, they'll already be onboard."

"Why would they be willing to take action on a gut feeling with no proof?"

"Two reasons. One, a legitimate concern backed by considerable circumstantial evidence, and two. I may be a corporate lawyer, but

I'm still a lawyer. That counts for something in certain circles," Blaine responded with a grim look.

"Thanks, man. I'm glad you're here. You go ahead and do what you have to do, and Joyce and I will look for Candace."

Chapter 29

They found her car parked at the site Rick had given him, but Candace was nowhere to be seen. Joyce was right—it was a seedy part of town, a place where drug addicts, drunks, and criminals resided. Candace would have no reason to be there. Joyce called her cell phone again, and this time they could hear a ringtone coming from somewhere inside the car. She took an extra set of keys from her purse and unlocked the door. They found Candace's phone, purse, and the tracking bracelet all lying in a pile on the passenger seat.

Brice's heart clinched with unspeakable fear. When he examined the bracelet, he could see that the clasp was twisted and broken, as though it had been ripped from her arm. She had certainly been taken against her will, and Brice had no doubt Nash was involved. Her car had been purposely left in this godforsaken part of town to be stolen, vandalized, or picked apart, to leave nothing of value behind.

"Where is she?" Joyce's fear was palpable.

"I don't know, but we're going to find her." Brice scanned the dilapidated buildings and surroundings with an uneasy feeling. "We need to get out of this area, fast, but we can't just leave her car here to be stripped. The police may want to go through it later to look for evidence. I want you to get in her car and drive it home. Try not to touch anything. I'll take it from here and call you when I have more news."

Joyce hesitated and studied his face with troubled eyes.

"Go on, do as I say, and don't worry. I promise you, I'm going to find her." He hugged her hard before letting her leave. Then he got into his own vehicle and called Rick.

"She's not here. Her car was empty and parked on the street in a very bad part of town. The bracelet and her other personal effects were left inside. I need you to initiate backup plan B. Once you have the new location, I want you to meet me there. I'll contact Blaine and keep him updated."

Brice stayed on the line and waited for the new coordinates. He'd always been a cautious man, and had backup plans for his backup plans. This was especially true when it involved the safety of the woman he loved. He'd gone a step further and had Candace's anklet fitted with a tracking device at the same time he'd had the bracelet fitted. Given that it was a smaller, more intricate piece of jewelry, Rick had replicated it and had turned the entire piece into an electronic tracking mechanism, like something straight out of a James Bond movie. Brice knew she never took it off. It had become so much a part of her that it could go virtually unnoticed. He was counting on it.

. . .

They all arrived at the new location—Brice, Rick, and, thanks to Blaine, a small contingent of the city of Atlanta Police Department's finest as backup. Blaine had managed to convince the DA's office that their support might be warranted. Of course, mentioning that the concerned party was the son of a former U.S. Ambassador didn't hurt either.

The site was a small, nondescript housing complex on the east side of town, several miles from where her car had been found. The team set up surveillance a short distance away and watched for movement inside and outside of the house. The police blocked off all incoming traffic and began formulating a plan to gain entrance, while Rick used the tracking device to pinpoint her location within the house.

If, as the device indicated, Candace was inside, the extraction had to pose as little danger to her as possible. They were still considering options when a pizza delivery car pulled up to the blocked entry. Officers questioned who the delivery was for and learned it was intended for the very house they were setting up watch on. After drawing up a hasty plan, one of the policemen exchanged places with the driver. He pulled on his cap and jacket, and drove his car through the blockade. He was preceded by a SWAT team on foot who took up positions on either side of the door. Brice was adamant that he be allowed to join them, but for safety concerns he was ordered to remain behind the barrier.

The "delivery boy" rang the doorbell and waited.

"What the hell took you so long? I've been waiting for forty-five minutes. Your promo says you'll deliver in thirty minutes or less, or I pay half. Well guess what, buddy? You get exactly half and no tip."

"Sorry, sir. There was a traffic delay a ways up the road. Somebody had an accident."

While Nash dug through his wallet, the policeman scanned the room behind him. He took the money and handed over the pizza, then touched the bill of his ball cap as the prearranged signal for the takedown. Suddenly, Nash was rushed by four armed SWAT team members, who pushed him onto the floor and handcuffed him before he could utter another word. He was taken down without a fight and trussed up like a prize pig at the county fair, ready for roasting. The only thing missing was an apple stuffed in his mouth.

Brice pushed through the containment line and rushed into the house. Candace was found in one of the bedrooms, her limp body sprawled face down across the mattress. His heart pumped wildly at the sight of her. He hurried to the bed and cradled her in his arms. He tenderly planted butterfly kisses on her lips and cheeks and gently patted her face. Her skin was pale and cool to his touch.

"Candace? Baby, wake up." She didn't respond. "Come on baby, it's Brice. Wake up now."

The EMTs arrived and firmly moved him aside to check her vital signs and administer first aid. Next to the bed were a syringe and a small vial of liquid, which the medics immediately checked. The bottle was three quarters full.

"Her heartbeat is irregular, and her breathing is too shallow." The EMT hurriedly put a respirator mask over her face.

"Her pulse is extremely weak, too."

"We've got to get fluids into her and get her in the wagon, stat."

Brice watched and listened as the two worked to revive Candace. The urgency with which they operated terrified him. He was choking on mixed emotions of anger, fear, and self-recrimination. This wasn't supposed to happen. He was supposed to protect her and keep her safe. He'd failed. She meant the world to him, and he didn't know what he'd do if he lost her.

Terror turned into rage and he rushed into the outer room. Nash stood between two police officers, his hands cuffed, and each man gripping an arm.

"You bastard! What did you give her?"

Nash remained silent, his mouth curved upward in a contemptuous smile. Furious, Brice streaked across the room and, ignoring the two officers, punched him right in the face, knocking him over backwards. He fell on top of him, intent on turning his body into a punching bag, but the remaining officers lunged forward and pulled him off before he could do more damage.

"You'd better pray to God she comes out of this okay!" he shouted. "If anything happens to her, you're a dead man."

Nash was pulled to his feet, bleeding from his mouth and nose, his sneering smile noticeably missing. His top lip was busted, and his nose was bent to one side, probably broken. "Are you going to let him get away with that? He assaulted me!"

"Assaulted? Did you see anyone assaulted, Ted?" one of the officers holding onto Nash asked the other.

"No." Ted shook his head solemnly. "I didn't see any assault. I saw Mr. Nash here trip and take a header off the top step. It was a nasty fall."

"We'll see what my lawyer has to say about this," Nash snarled. "The press is going to have a field day. When I'm done, you jerks won't be laughing then."

Brice shook himself free of the other officer's hold and leaned over and breathed in Nash's face with unbridled contempt. "In case you haven't noticed, dickhead, you've got bigger problems to worry about. Kidnapping is a serious offense, you crazy, arrogant fuck. And this time there won't be anyone to make the charges disappear. You're going to jail. You're going to jail for a very long time."

Chapter 30

Doctors and nurses rushed from every direction to meet the ambulance when it arrived, and Candace was immediately taken into the emergency room. Against his will, Brice was forced to wait outside to answer questions and deal with admittance paperwork. It felt like hours before a doctor came out to speak with him, and the news caused his heart to drop straight into his shoes.

"She's still unconscious. Her breathing is shallow, and her heart rate is practically nonexistent. We're flushing her system and trying to raise her blood pressure and pulse rate back to within normal levels. He gave her multiple intramuscular injections of Lorazepam, and it appears she might have had an allergic reaction. The drug alone is extremely powerful; the allergy complicates matters more and could cause respiratory failure. A few more hours and she could very well have died. The good news is we got to her in time. Currently her condition is grave, but she appears to be responding favorably. But I'm afraid that for now, all we can do is give it time and wait and see what happens."

Brice felt as though he'd been physically punched right in the chest. He found it hard to breathe with pain in his heart so severe and fear so strong; he was scared to death he was going to lose her. Even though the doctor's prognosis was promising, he didn't feel reassured. If she didn't come through this, he didn't know how he'd survive.

Word spread quickly that Candace had been found. The waiting room was in chaos as friends and family arrived, anxious for news. In typical fashion, Brice had lied about being her fiancé and had been allowed to stay by her side the entire time. He was there when her parents, Blaine and Joyce, Sarona and David, and a whole host of coworkers and acquaintances arrived. Now everyone waited and worried together over what the outcome would be. Her parents were led to the ER to see her, and Brice reluctantly stepped aside and went to join their friends.

Brice briefly filled them in and assured them that Nash had been taken away in handcuffs. Joyce hugged him tightly. "Thank God you found her in time."

"I let her down, Joyce. I let that crazy bastard get to her."

"How can you say that? If it weren't for you, that 'crazy bastard' might still be loose, and Candace could have been lost to us forever. You saved her, Brice, you and Blaine." She stretched out her hand to pull Blaine closer and took his hand in hers and squeezed it. "Thanks to the two of you, we have a reason to be grateful. We have our girl back."

Her parents returned to the waiting area, both in a state of shock. Brice, along with Joyce, went over to introduce himself. "Good evening, Mr. and Mrs. Brown. You don't know me, but my name is Brice Coleman, and I'm deeply in love with your daughter."

Eighteen hours later, her condition was downgraded from grave to "guarded," and she was turned over to general care. Brice made arrangements to have her placed in a private suite with an adjoining room for her family. He spent every moment sitting next to her bed, when he wasn't lying beside her and holding her, waiting for her to wake up.

• • •

She awoke to the sensation of warmth radiating from the body lying next to her, encircled in familiar arms and surrounded by the uniquely familiar fragrance of pure male. Her head was pillowed against a solid chest that rose and fell with every breath. She smiled at the reassuring sound of gentle snoring and snuggled in closer and breathed him in, imprinting on his scent. She knew this body ... this scent ... this man.

She remembered floating on a cloud of fantasy and drifting in and out of consciousness, unanchored in a place where time had no meaning. She remembered the sound of voices. So many voices. There were people everywhere. Only one persistent voice had penetrated her foggy mind, and she let it draw her back from the dark void. She'd fought her way back. To him. For him. The veil of fantasy and fog had been lifted. This wasn't a dream. This was real.

She laid her hand on his chest and lightly stroked it, tracing his masculine lines and drawing tiny circular patterns with her finger.

He stirred. His grip tightened, and he buried his face in her hair and brushed the top of her head with a kiss. "You're awake."

"No. I'm still dreaming."

"What are you dreaming about?"

"Knights in shining armor, handsome princes, and happily-ever-afters."

"Umm, I was hoping you were dreaming about me."

"I'm sure I would have gotten around to you, sooner or later." She chuckled softly, her lips pressed against his chest, savoring his warmth and the steady beat of his heart against her cheek.

He put his fingers under her chin and tilted her head back so he could gaze into her eyes.

"You scared the hell out of me and took ten years off my life. I almost lost you." He choked, and his voice filled with unchecked emotion. "I don't ever want to feel that way again." He tangled his hand in her hair, pulled her lips closer, and kissed her tenderly ... reverently, and poured everything he was into that one kiss. She tasted his fear, his ache, and his uncertainty. His emotions pulsed against her lips and washed over her in waves, and she felt the truth of his words down to her toes. When he finally pulled away, he put his forehead to hers and took a shaky breath.

"I'm never letting you go. Do you hear me? I don't care how hard you fight to get away from me. I love you, Candace, and no one will ever take you away from me again. I'm not pressuring you. I know you need time to figure things out and make up your mind, but just know that I'm not going anywhere. I'm in this for the duration." His voice dropped to little more than a whisper. "You already have *my* heart and soul. I'll wait for you to give me yours."

His gaze fell upon her bruised cheek, and he brushed it lightly with his fingertips. "He hurt you."

"He scared me."

"I wasn't there."

"I pushed you away."

She cupped his cheek in her hand and looked him in the eye. He looked exhausted. His long and shaggy hair hung over his eyes, and his face hadn't seen the sharp edge of a razor in at least a day or two. He'd never looked so rugged, or so tired. She combed his hair to the side with her fingers. Looked deeper, she saw more than fatigue below the surface. There was concern and love reflected back at her. Real, true love. Her heart clinched, and tears threatened to fill her eyes. She kissed him softly on his lips and then cuddled closer, again resting her head on his chest. She felt safe and comforted there. She threaded her fingers through his and pressed their entwined hands against her chest.

"You're wrong, Brice. You *were* with me, through every terrifying moment. You were there when I needed you most. And even though the experience was nothing I'd care to repeat in this lifetime, something good came from it. Nash, in his own twisted way, did what neither you nor Joyce were able to do. He opened my eyes and made me see what a fool I was. I'd let men like him get inside my head and make me believe that real love didn't really exist. That stuff like that only happened in fairy tales, or the movies. And I was okay with that, until you came along—you, with your sweet, protective, and caring ways that scared the crap out of me.

"You were too good to be true; therefore, everything about you had to be a lie. I'd settled for less for so long I was too afraid to hope for better. When Nash tried to belittle you and claimed he knew the kind of man you were, he made me realize how wrong we both were. I'd closed my mind to possibilities. Every time I said no to you, I was really saying no to me and denying myself the experience of something wonderful—some*one* wonderful."

She rose up on her elbow and looked him in the eyes again, filled with determination and conviction.

"I knew you'd come for me. It didn't matter that he'd taken the bracelet and made me leave everything behind. I knew you'd find me because ... I knew you loved me. I *was* dreaming about you, Brice," she confessed in a small voice. "You always come to my rescue, just like in all those fairy tales. You saved me from Nash, and you saved me from myself. *You* are my knight, my prince, and my ever after." She leaned over and kissed his lips. "Thank you."

He pulled her into his arms and crushed her against him until she felt him tremble. She let him hold her, even if his grip was a little tight. She sensed his need to. When he was finally able to let go, he brushed her hair back from her face and smiled down at her.

"I have something for you. I've held onto it for weeks, hoping and waiting for the right moment." He pulled a small black velvet box from his jacket pocket and gave it to her. She opened it and was stunned to see nestled inside a beautiful princess-cut diamond ring in a platinum setting. He removed the ring and carefully slipped it onto her finger. It fit perfectly and looked as though it had always belonged there.

"I know this is sudden and unexpected, and that you're still trying to find your way. But I don't need months and months to think and analyze what I'm feeling inside. I already know where my heart belongs. It belongs to you." He brought her hand to his lips and brushed it with a kiss. "You don't have to say yes right now. Just don't say no."

She stared at the ring in silent wonder, absorbing the proof of his love there on her finger, and her hand shook under the weight of all that it implied. The tears that had threatened for so long finally spilled over and tracked down her face, and he leaned over and gently kissed them away. She closed her eyes and wrapped her arms around his neck.

"I was so determined not to fall in love with you, Brice. But I'm glad I have crappy willpower."

The last brick in her wall crumbled and fell. She no longer needed her shield to protect herself. She'd finally let go of the past and allowed herself to believe that her heart and her future were in good hands.

Epilogue

Three months later

"Wake up, sleepyhead." He rolled her over and nuzzled her neck. One hand rested on her bare breast while the other supported her head and pulled her closer for a kiss. After all this time, he was still in awe that he was allowed to live and breathe and wake up next to this woman. It had been months since the kidnapping, but he still hadn't gotten past the fear of almost losing her. There were nights he'd jerk awake in a panic from dreams that Nash had gotten away with his plan or that he hadn't found her in time. He'd reach out and pull her close and breathe away his fear and reassure himself she really was all right. He knew that deep down he'd never get over that feeling of terror.

That day in the hospital when he'd given her the ring, when, to his surprise, she'd said yes, that guarded look of distrust and fear had been replaced by something new—determination, devotion, and love. Andrew Nash could rot in jail for all he cared, but he grudgingly owed him a debt of thanks. If not for his dramatic actions, Candace might never have come to the conclusion that Brice really loved her. Now she belonged to him, body, heart, and soul.

His parents had fallen in love with her on sight, and she and his mother had quickly become friends. His only hope was that she didn't scare Candace off with all her badgering about how soon they planned to start having babies. His mom had a one-track mind.

"Who's asleep? I've been lying here waiting patiently for *you* to wake up so I could jump your bones."

"Why'd you wait, babe? You know you don't need an invitation. You can jump my bones anytime and anywhere." His voice was low and wickedly sensual.

"Really? Anywhere?" Her eyes stretched wide and sparkled with mock amazement and mischief.

He felt that familiar punched-in-the-gut feeling he always got when he looked into that beautiful sparkling well of brown and golden flecks.

"Don't act like you're surprised. I think it's safe to say that our escapade in the elevator more than justifies that statement. Not to mention the kitchen counter, the dining room table—and let us not forget the hot tub in the backyard. If you want to try something different, why don't we stay in the bed for a change?" He chuckled.

"You must have been reading my mind." She grinned as she reached down and wrapped her hand around his shaft and felt it pulse and come alive in her palm. She gripped it firmly and stroked the length of it, letting her thumb slide across the head and make tiny circles over the tip. He groaned his pleasure, enjoying her soft touch. She leaned in and traced his lips with her tongue, insisting he open for her, and he complied. Once the kiss started, he took over and dominated her, taking it deep. He pulled her head back and skimmed her throat with his lips and tongue, and then spoke into her neck, his breath warm against her skin.

"Don't you have somewhere to be?" he asked.

"Mm hmm."

"You know, if you start this, I'm not letting you out of this bed until we're finished."

"So, stop talking." She breathed in his ear. "Time's a-wasting."

"I'm just giving you fair warning, babe." He covered her mouth with his, and in one swift move he flipped over onto his back and pulled her on top of him. She spread her legs, opening wide to allow his cock easy access to slide inside her wet, warm channel. The sensation made them both shudder and groan with pleasure, and they were immediately swept away and lost inside their self-made world of love and lust.

• • •

She raised her head and looked at the clock on the dresser, and her eyes grew wide with alarm. "Damn it. Look what you've done. I'm going to be late! Sarona and Joyce are going to *kill* me." She jumped out of bed and hurriedly gathered her things. "They warned me not to spend the night with you because they knew this would happen. I can just see them now, tapping their feet and checking their watches. I'll have to listen to them muttering 'I told you so' for the rest of the day."

Brice looked at her with a satisfied grin. She might be frantic, but he was feeling pretty damn good.

"Hey, don't blame me. I warned you."

"I am not taking all the blame for this, mister. If I go down, you're going down with me. Don't just lie there. Get up! We've got a wedding to go to!"

"Go ahead and get in the shower. I'd join you, but we both know I won't be able to keep my hands off of you. I'd only make you later than you already are. I've got a little more time than you."

"Yeah, you're right." She gave him a hurried kiss on the lips and rushed into the bathroom to take a quick shower and dress.

He lay back with his fingers laced together behind his head, grinning like an idiot as he stared at the ceiling. He felt like the luckiest man in the world. The woman he loved was only a few feet away, and very soon, she'd be a permanent fixture in his life and in his home.

• • •

The wedding march sounded, and all heads turned to watch the bride's approach. The groom was nervous but proud and sported a grin across his face from ear to ear. The bride was led down the aisle on the arm of her father, who smiled and proudly delivered her into the hands of her husband-to-be. When she took her place among the group, they stood in a row in front of the altar, the six of them, all friends. They had come together in a time of trouble and near loss, and now they stood together in a time of joy to bear witness to the blending of friendships and families. This union would make the bond between them tighter, stronger.

Brice looked across the narrow space that separated them all, and then stared at Candace. Her transformation from tousled lover to elegant beauty was breathtaking. She was the product of that wonderful magic women worked when the occasion called for something special. He couldn't take his eyes off of her. The love he felt welled up inside and threatened to overflow, and he was completely consumed by a tidal wave of emotion. During the course of the ceremony, the minister's voice resonated throughout the church as he spoke in reverent tones. But Brice was so focused on her face, her lips, and her eyes that the words were lost to him.

David poked him in the ribs. "Hey," he whispered loudly, his voice rippling with repressed laughter. "Pay attention. Your turn will come soon enough."

The minister repeated his question. "May we have the ring, please?" Brice grinned sheepishly and reached into his inside pocket to retrieve the wedding band and handed it to David. David turned and smiled at his lovely bride and repeated his wedding vow in a clear, strong voice. Brice listened to the words of commitment as he looked meaningfully at Candace, and she returned his stare with a look of understanding.

David was right; their turn would come soon enough. They had come a long way together. The evil villain had been thwarted, the beautiful maiden had been rescued, and the hero had gotten the girl. It was a happily-ever-after ending ... after all.

More from This Author
(From *Prelude to a Seduction* by Lotchie Burton)

"What are you doing?"

"I'm undressing you," he murmurs, as his fingers deftly unfasten the buttons of her blouse and unzip her skirt. His mouth teases and nibbles at her neck and shoulder.

"Silly man, of course you're undressing me." She giggles. "Maybe my question should have been, Why?"

"Because," he whispers in her ear and lets his lips journey down her cheek to trail kisses across her chin and lips. "I love to touch your skin, and I can't touch you with all these clothes on."

Her smile is warm and sexy; her breath is hot and sweet. "I know, but if you keep this up, I'll never get out of here on time."

"That's the plan," he says, showing off perfect, beautiful white teeth in a wide, wolfish grin.

"I can't be late, not again!" She shrieks with laughter when he leans forward and licks that elusive sensitive spot just behind her ear.

"I'll bet no one will even notice. Come on, babe, let me send you off with a smile on your face," he cajoles. "Or at least let me send you off with a smile on my face." He grins and wiggles his eyebrows up and down. She shakes her head. He knows she'll eventually give up and give in to his persuasive mouth and convincing hands. Ignoring her feeble attempts at protest, he continues to methodically strip her clothing away piece by piece until she stands completely naked and exposed to his appraising gaze. He lays her down upon the bed and blankets her with his body, burying his face between her soft, succulent breasts.

"Mm," he sighs in muffled contentment. "You feel so soft. I could lie here forever."

"We don't have forever," she purrs seductively, "and I can't wait that long. You've got me naked; you need to do something about it right now."

"I'm more than happy to oblige, my lady," he responds, his voice low and husky with need. "Your demand is my wish." He brushes and strokes her body with nimble fingers and knowledgeable hands, familiar with every curve, every dip, and every hollow. He knows her body in intimate detail, and he knows what it takes to make her hum, purr, and sing for him.

"I love the way you smell. You smell like ice cream," he murmurs and slowly kisses and licks his way down the length of her body.

"Ice cream?"

"Yeah, ice cream. I want to see if you taste like ice cream, too." He reaches his destination and settles himself between her legs, at the juncture where her silky smooth thighs spread and separate, and allow him access to her liquid heat. He pushes his face down into her heated crevice, inhaling deeply and drawing in the distinctly musky, sweet scent of her sex. His tongue flicks and licks and laps and tastes the gathering pool of nectar, generated by his skillful touch.

"You taste like caramel, like caramel over ice cream," he whispers against her sensitive bud. "Mmmm, you're so sweet. I can never get enough of your taste." He continues to stroke her silken walls with his tongue and to tease her hidden pearl; then he dips deep inside to taste more of her. She moans and writhes from the pleasure.

"Oh, babe, it feels so good, but I want to feel you inside me. I need to have your hard, throbbing cock here." She uses her hand to point the way. "Inside me now."

He shudders with his desire and rises to fulfill her urgent plea. He pushes her legs higher, spreads them wider, moving into position to plunge deep. Her moans excite him and stir and push him toward the edge. He presses the tip of his shaft at her entrance, anxious and impatient to feel her hot, velvet sheath wrapped and squeezing tightly around his —

BEEP! BEEP! BEEP!

David's eyes flew open to the recognizable sound of the alarm clock incessantly beeping, the noise loud enough to wake the dead. He came fully awake, his body taut, rigid, and aching with a raging hard-on, his cock hard enough to punch through steel. Damn! It was another damn dream! He groaned and angrily slapped the off button on his clock. Closing his eyes and resting his head against the headboard, he tried to breathe through his painful erection, knowing the feeling would subside as the memory of the dream faded. Unable to completely quell the desire that constantly rode him, he punched the pillow in utter frustration, hard, hot, and achingly unfulfilled.

In the mood for more Crimson Romance?
Check out *The Real Thing* by Susann Oriel
at *CrimsonRomance.com*.

Printed in the United States
By Bookmasters